Date Due

SE 1 9 08			
OC 0 9 08			
MR 2 0 09			
4 2 5 0			
0 2 2			
SE 2 3 11			
SE 1 8 14			
SE 1 8 14			

BRODART, INC.   Cat. No. 23 233   Printed in U.S.A.

How I Saved My Father's Life

(AND RUINED EVERYTHING ELSE)

How I Saved My Father's Life

(AND RUINED EVERYTHING ELSE)

ANN HOOD

SCHOLASTIC PRESS/NEW YORK — An Imprint of Scholastic Inc.

Acknowledgments

I WOULD LIKE TO THANK SAM AND ARIANE ADRAIN, THE YOUNG ADULTS IN MY LIFE, FOR INSPIRING ME TO WRITE A BOOK THAT THEY WOULD WANT TO READ; LINDSAY WALLER FOR READING THE MANUSCRIPT EARLY ON AND BRAINSTORMING TITLES FOR ME; MY AGENT, GAIL HOCHMAN, FOR ENCOURAGING ME TO WRITE THIS; MY MOST FABULOUS EDITOR, FRANCESCO SEDITA, WHO ACTUALLY MADE THE EDITING PROCESS FUN AND WHOSE ENTHUSIASM IS BOUNDLESS; AND MY DARLING HUSBAND, LORNE ADRAIN, WHO LETS ME DISAPPEAR INTO MY STUDY FOR HOURS ON END AND DO WHAT I LOVE TO DO—WRITE.

Library of Congress Cataloging-in-Publication Data

Hood, Ann, 1956–

How I saved my father's life (and ruined everything else) / by Ann Hood.—1st ed.

p. cm.

Summary: After her father leaves and marries the glamorous Ava Pomme, Madeline blames her mother for their difficult new life, but in spite of the twelve-year-old's efforts to achieve sainthood, it takes a summer trip to Italy to put her family into perspective.

ISBN-13: 978-0-439-92819-9 (hardcover)

ISBN-10: 0-439-92819-2 (hardcover)

[1. Divorce—Fiction.   2. Remarriage—Fiction.   3. Family life—Rhode Island—Fiction.
4. Catholic Church—Fiction.   5. Rhode Island—Fiction.   6. Italy—Fiction.]   I. Title.

PZ7.H7627Ho 2008

[Fic]—dc22

2007010868

10 9 8 7 6 5 4 3 2 1   08 09 10 11 12

Printed in the U.S.A. • 23 • Reinforced Binding for Library Use

Book design by Kristina Albertson

First edition, March 2008

For Sam

Chapter One

AVALANCHE

MY NAME IS MADELINE VANDERMEER and this is the story about the year that I wanted to become a saint. Don't get the wrong idea. I'm not a religious fanatic or anything. I'm not even a religious person. My family never goes to church, or says prayers before bed. But things happened in my life that led me to believe I could be a saint. Maybe even *should* be a saint. I actually performed two miracles. Before this, I was a normal kid in a normal family. At least, we were sort of normal. When I was little, we lived in Boston in a neighborhood called Back Bay. Our brownstone was connected to a bunch of others, all lined up in a pretty row. We were the third house from the left — my mother, Alice; my father, Scott; me; and later my baby brother, Cody.

Both of my parents are writers, and when we lived in Boston, even though we were happy and did happy things like play Uno and make banana splits and take walks in the Public Gardens together, we were also always broke. *Writers' incomes fluctuate very much,* my parents always used to say. When I was ten, their incomes fluctuated way down and we left Boston and moved one hour south to Providence, Rhode Island. Providence is the capital of Rhode Island, but it hardly looks like a city at all. There are only five tall buildings, and one of them is a hotel, not even a real skyscraper. Boston has beautiful tall buildings made out of glass that shine in the sunlight, and it has traffic and crowds on the streets. To me, these are the things that make a city.

But in Providence, people live in houses with yards and sometimes you can walk down the street and pass maybe an old lady walking her dog or a couple of Brown University students rushing to class. In Boston, I wasn't allowed to roam around. But in Providence, as long as I let my mother know I'm leaving, I can walk down to Thayer Street and get a falafel at East Side Pockets or just look in the store windows or go and sit on the Brown green and pretend I am in college.

Not too long after we moved, my father got an assignment to write about heli-skiing in Idaho. This is when adventurous people let a helicopter drop them off on some remote mountain and then they ski down it. My father is adventurous. He is handsome and charming and smart. Back then, I used to think my mother was pretty great, too. She would rub my back if I couldn't fall asleep and sometimes we would play Beauty Parlor and paint each other's toenails in our favorite color, Melon of Troy. "Puns are the lowest form of humor," my mother always said when she pulled out that bottle of nail polish. We loved that silly name, Melon of Troy.

My two miracles both happened over a year ago, when I turned eleven. That winter was the last time my mother made me a birthday cake shaped like a snowman—covered in gooey white frosting, sprinkled coconut, black gumdrop eyes, and a black licorice mouth. It was the last time it snowed on my birthday, too—December 19. That season I was in a special performance of the Boston Ballet's *The Nutcracker*. I didn't have the role I wanted exactly, but some kids didn't get any part at all so I was happy to have made it. Plus I got to wear the glitteriest costume ever. My father said I glittered all the way across the auditorium.

The week before my birthday, on December 12, the date of Miracle Number One, I made a glass of water slide across the kitchen table and smash onto the floor all by itself. I did it just by staring. I stared and stared at it, imagining it skating across the smooth surface, actually seeing in my mind the way it would teeter at the edge before crashing down, sending a spray of water across the floor. I stared at that glass, and pictured it falling, until it finally did. A miracle. And since I made one miracle happen, I had to try for more. So I attempted to make a drawer slam shut on its own, a light go dim or even flicker a little, the bathtub faucet turn itself on and then off. Things like that. But nothing worked.

I almost gave up. At night, I prayed into the darkness: "Please give me special powers. Please, please, please." I don't know any official prayers, just a Cherokee chant and things like that, which I threw in for good measure. What had I done exactly right in that moment? Was there something special about the kitchen? Or was it the time of day? I thought about that glass sliding across the kitchen table, the way it glissaded as if it took ballet from Madame Natasha at the

Ballet School, too. The Ballet School was in Boston and every Saturday my mother drove me to my class there, even though it was an hour away. Not only did kids from the Ballet School get to try out for *The Nutcracker*, we also had the best chance of getting into the Boston Ballet's junior company. So even after we moved to Providence I got to take my class there with Madame.

I decided that to perform more miracles maybe I needed to be in the kitchen, so I moved all of my efforts downstairs, and waited until the afternoon light sent rays of amber and violet at just the right slant through the stained glass window above the stairs. Then I sat and stared. At the sink with its white and silver old-fashioned knobs that said HOT and COLD; at the only drawer that didn't stick in our new house (new to us, that is; it's actually really an old, old house); at the bare bulb that hung over the kitchen table, the one that first had a long string hanging from it and then, because it still wasn't long enough for me or Cody to reach, also had a coat hanger covered in the fuzzy pink sash of my mother's old bathrobe.

According to my mother, someday we would get enough money to fix the house up and make it beautiful, like the other houses in our neighborhood. Those other houses had polished wood floors instead of scuffed-up ones like ours and lights that were covered up and walls painted clean white or rich deep colors like dark red or Christmas green. This house was an embarrassment. Right in the next yard, there was a fancy, elaborate play set, with colorful tunnels that led to curly slides and a small rope bridge and lots of swings and a Tarzan rope that swung across a goldfish pond.

The girl who owned that play set was named Sophie and she was beautiful, with straight blond hair always held off her face with a different headband: checks or stripes or solid colors topped with a small bow. I didn't have very many friends in Providence, and the ones I did have felt like friends of convenience. Like the daughters of women my mother was friends with, or other new kids, or Mai Mai Fan from school who was so busy being a chess champion that she was willing to be anybody's friend because she could never actually do anything like go for pizza or watch DVDs. The only reason why Sophie was my friend was because she lived next door and sometimes got so bored she actually invited me over. And even though I didn't like her too much, I went. Sometimes, we even had fun together. But not usually. Whenever I told my mother I was going over to Sophie's she would say, "But I thought you didn't like Sophie," and I would just shrug. Our relationship was complicated.

Sophie was beautiful. I am not beautiful. My mother said I would grow into my looks, the way she also says I will grow into my too-big winter coat and the sweatshirt that I have to roll up the sleeves of whenever I need to use my hands. Madame said I am unusual-looking. "This is good for the ballet," Madame said. Which I guess means not good for all the other parts of my life. My hair is coarse like straw and the same color. If I push it behind my ears, they stick out like the ones you screw on Mr. Potato Head. My nose has nostrils like a horse's, long and narrow. They flare whenever I get angry, which is pretty often lately. My lips are long and narrow, too. My mother has those lips. The nostrils come from my father's side; all of his sisters have them.

What I do have are beautiful, perfect ballerina feet: high arched. I can jump better than anyone at the Ballet School. My feet, lovely and shaped like the arched bridge on the Brio train set that Cody wanted for Christmas, are my best asset. An asset that no one can see. So I go barefoot whenever I can so people can see them and admire them. I can stand very erect and lift one leg so that it reaches my face, and flex my beautiful toes, in case someone hadn't noticed.

That winter, whenever I wasn't experimenting with my powers, I stood outside in my leg warmers and that too-big — "It'll last for years and then Cody will wear it, too!" — cherry-red down jacket, my fuzzy hot-pink earmuffs, the purple and black and green mittens my father brought me from Ecuador, one blue snow boot, and one bare perfect foot that I brought carefully up to my face and then flexed, over and over. My breath came out in small puffs and my nose ran. But I didn't care. Some things I did for God. Other things I did for art. I wondered if the library had some kind of list of saints and what they had suffered for, beside the obvious stuff like world peace and justice for the poor. Maybe I would become the first saint who was a ballerina.

"That's totally weird," Sophie said from her yard.

She was peering through a hole in the fence that separated the two properties. It was my parents' responsibility to fix that hole, but they had no intention of doing that when they needed new plumbing and rewiring, not to mention having the floors sanded and polished, the walls painted, and insulation installed.

I didn't answer. For one thing, I hated her something fierce, standing there with her headband and private school uniform. For another, the flexing kept my foot from going numb and I needed to concentrate.

"It's like five degrees out here and you're barefoot," Sophie said. As if I didn't know I was barefoot.

"Really, Sophie? I'm barefoot? Thanks for that information. Why don't you go and brush your hair a hundred times or something?" I said, watching my breath come out in little clouds, like smoke.

"My mother still can't believe someone bought this dump," Sophie said.

I squinted toward her, trying to maintain my concentration.

"It has character," I said. It's one thing for me to say our house was a dump, but when Sophie said it I wanted to kill her.

"They couldn't sell it, you know. They lived there for like forty years and never lifted a finger. The man, Mr. Greer, died inside." Then she added in a whisper, "Of cancer."

Now I searched the hole until I found a piece of Sophie's face—one eye and her nose. Nothing was worse than Sophie having important information that I didn't have, especially about my very own house. "In the kitchen?" I asked her. Of course I was trying to sound disinterested, but really the possibilities thrilled me. Maybe the kitchen *was* the source of power in the house. Maybe every miracle I performed would originate from there. Maybe a ghost was helping me with my miracles!

"I don't know," Sophie said. "He had hospice."

I frowned and memorized the word to look up later. Even though my parents were writers, whenever I asked them what a word meant they said, "Look it up." I always said, "But how am I going to do that when I don't even know how to spell it?" "Trial and error," my father would say. One of my parents' prized possessions was their *Oxford English Dictionary*, which stood in the middle of our living room like another member of the family on its own library stand.

"You," Sophie said, snapping me out of my thoughts, "are, like, crazy."

"And you say *like* too much," I said. "My parents charge me a dime every time I use *like* inappropriately. Your parents should do the same. They would be rich by now."

"They're already rich," Sophie said so matter-of-factly, I wanted to kill her all over again.

"Good for them," I said. I suppose Sophie had drawers full of Fruity Punch Lip Smackers. Closets full, even.

"Are you li—" Sophie stopped herself and I smirked, right in her direction. "Are you a ballerina or something?"

"I was in the Boston Ballet's production of Tchaikovsky's *The Nutcracker*," I kind of lied. I mean, my performance was with the official company. Did Sophie have to know that it was just one special performance and not the official show? After all, she had so much to brag about and sometimes she made me feel terrible. Surely a little white lie didn't matter?

"But I saw that!" Sophie said while I searched my conscience. "Why wouldn't you tell me if you were in it? I'm sure you weren't in it."

"I was, too!" I shouted. "I didn't tell you because we haven't hung out in a long time," I said hoping she might feel badly about that.

That *was* the truth, and it was probably why I felt mad at her. Her family went skiing over Thanksgiving break, somewhere fancy with perfect snow. When we moved here three months ago, she actually came over with a stupid T-shirt for me that said: *Watch out where them Huskies go, Don't you eat that yellow snow.*

Sophie considered my white lie. "Were you Clara?" she said finally.

"I was a Spanish dancer," I said, which was true, and when she looked smug I said, "Next year I'll be Clara," with more certainty than I really felt. "I have perfect ballerina feet."

Sophie pressed her face against the hole for a better look.

"Like Marie Taglioni," I added.

No way did Sophie know who that was. It was my mother who introduced me to Marie Taglioni. For my eighth birthday she gave me a book called *Great Ballerinas* and we both fell in love with Marie Taglioni above all of the others. *Born, 1804; died, 1884; created a delicate new style marked by floating leaps and balanced poses, such as the arabesque.* I was already taking ballet classes then, but we were little and just ran around for half an hour while the teacher yelled, "Be a tree!" and we'd all strike a pose like weeping willows or giant oaks. Sometimes we would lie on the floor and bend ourselves into shapes like the alphabet. But after my mother gave me that book and we read about Marie Taglioni, all I wanted was to do floating leaps and arabesques, just like her.

"Madeline," my mother called from the porch, "it's time!"

"I have to go," I said, relieved. "My father's going to Idaho and we're all taking him to the airport."

Taking Dad to the airport meant lunch at Durkin's Park first. My father and I always got the Yankee pot roast. I hopped across the patches of snow in the yard so my foot would stay dry.

"I don't think you were in *The Nutcracker*," Sophie said. "I still have my program. I'm going to look."

"Be my guest," I said to Sophie.

Hospice, I said to myself. After we got back from Boston, I would add it to my New Vocabulary list and then I would call Mai Mai Fan and tell her that my list finally had 100 words. By the time we got in our decrepit Volvo to drive to Logan Airport, I had practically wiped Sophie from my mind.

Every night while my father was away in Idaho, my mother and Cody and I watched the Weather Channel. Snow always hung right over Idaho. It was funny that my father had gone to a place called Sun Valley in a state that clearly never got any sun.

The night that I saved my father's life, Cody fell asleep right in front of the TV while we waited for the Idaho weather. I sat on the couch, trying to drink from a straw while I was lying down so that if I ever became paralyzed or got a terminal disease, I would still be able to drink coffee milk, my favorite thing in the world, and one of the only good things available here in Providence but nowhere else in the country, maybe even the entire universe. My mother was reading a book and taking notes for an article about healthy eating.

She looked up at me and said, "Why are you wearing that ridiculous Husky T-shirt?"

I grinned, loving her so much for that.

"Let's put it in the giveaway bin," she said. The giveaway bin was where clothes that didn't even fit Cody ended up.

"Look," I said, pointing to the television, "there's Idaho."

"More snow," Cody said.

I tried to imagine my father riding in a helicopter and getting dropped off on some mountain, having to find his way back. He was, I knew, resourceful. After all, he had climbed all the way to the top of Mount Kilimanjaro. He had eaten a roasted guinea pig in Quito, which is the capital of Ecuador. He had ridden on a raft down the Amazon River while guerrillas shot at him. But still, finding your way off a mountain in the snow in Idaho sounded really scary.

"What if Daddy doesn't find his way off that mountain?" I asked my mother.

"He will," she said without looking up.

"How do you know?"

"He's with a guide, for one thing."

I sighed and watched the weather report for the Cape and islands. Rain. Cody thought that was a special place, *the Capon Islands*, even though our father had shown him on a map and everything: Cape Cod and the islands, Martha's Vineyard and Nantucket.

"Have I ever been to Nantucket?" I asked my mother.

"When you were a baby."

That made me smile. I loved to think of myself as a baby, a bald pink thing that was carried from place to place, Nantucket and Mexico and London and Barbados, in some kind of conscious state; I remembered none of it. In pictures, I look so cute in my jean jacket and OshKosh overalls, with ridiculous droopy hats.

"I wish I could remember," I said.

"All you need to know," she told me, "is that you were the most fabulous, most adored, most wonderful baby ever." She smiled at me.

Even though I had just turned eleven, I wanted to curl up right on her lap and stay there for a while. Before the divorce, my mother had that effect on me.

Instead, I asked her, "What's hospice?"

She looked up, all worried. "It's where people go when they're dying, when there's no hope for them at all. Who's in hospice?"

"It's a place?" I asked, disappointed, thinking that Mr. Greer maybe didn't die in the kitchen after all. Then where was my source of power? And how would I ever find it again?

"Yes. Well, yes and no," she explained. "Hospice workers sometimes go to the person's house and help take care of them until they die. Like Boppa."

Boppa was my father's father, a heart surgeon, a smart man who nonetheless died last year of the same disease a famous baseball player named Lou Gehrig died from. After Boppa got that disease, my father made us all watch that movie so we'd understand better. Then Boppa died, and that's how we got money to buy this house.

My mother was going on and on about Boppa and the nurses that stayed with him around the clock and how that way everybody got to be right with him when he died.

Lucky everybody, I thought, shivering. I had never seen a dead person and I didn't want to.

"And he got to die at home," my mother continued, "right where he wanted."

Lucky Boppa, I thought, already bored with hospice. Maybe I wouldn't add hospice to my New Vocabulary list after all.

My mother sighed and looked dreamy. I wondered if she was thinking of her own father who had also died, but without hospice. He just lay down for a nap one Saturday afternoon and died.

She stood then and scooped sleeping Cody up in her arms. "Want to join us?" she asked.

Every time our father was away on an assignment, Cody always slept with our mother. I used to, too, the three of us i my parents' big bed, with the smell of freshly

 d pencils and Secret deodorant in the air. But Cody

 ook up too much room with his flailing arms, his need to always have the cool side of his pillow up, and his screams in the middle of the night from stupid nightmares.

I almost said yes. But shouldn't an eleven-year-old *not* want to sleep with her mother and her little brother?

"No, thanks," I said. "I think I'll stay up really late and watch television."

She smiled and kissed me good night. "Not too late," she said.

After they went upstairs, I tried to find something on television that I wasn't allowed to watch, but there was nothing good on and I fell asleep with the TV right back on the Weather Channel. At some point, I got up and climbed into my own bed and thought about Marie Taglioni and hospice and the snow in Idaho until the next thing I knew I was startled awake by a man's voice saying my name as clear as anything: "Madeline. Madeline."

I sat up.

I waited.

"Mr. Greer?" I said, because who else could it be?

The clock by my bedside seemed to tick extra loud. It was three o'clock.

I waited, but the man didn't speak again. My heart was pounding against my ribs. I was terrified. I was exhilarated. I got out of bed, my knees all trembly. The floor was cold but I didn't even stop to put on my father's rag socks, the ones I wore as slippers. Instead, I went straight over to the window, uncertain what drew me there. When I parted the lace curtains — left behind by the Greers — and looked out, all I saw was a blanket of snow. Snow so thick I could not make out anything, not the street or Sophie's house next door. Even the light from the streetlamps was dim, a distant creepy glow.

I waited by the window until I got too sleepy to stand there any longer. Then I went back to bed, puzzled. My heart was still beating faster than usual, but my curiosity took over. *What did Mr. Greer want to show me?* I wondered. But then I fell right back asleep, easy as anything, and dreamed of snow falling on a mountainside in huge flakes, flakes the size and shape of Idaho, like crooked triangles. They fell and covered everything in their path — trees and SnoCats and skiers.

Skiers! My father! Something wasn't right, I thought with a start and pulled myself right out of that dream until I was wide awake.

It was morning. On our block the sun was shining brightly. Ice had formed around the tree branches, and the street outside my bedroom window glistened like a fairy-tale forest. It was kind of like rock candy had taken over everything. The snow in the street looked like a beautiful white blanket, without even one footprint in it. I remembered how Sophie had bragged about the snow wherever she had gone skiing at Thanksgiving. "We were the very first people to touch that snow, Madeline," she'd said. Now I knew what she meant. I dressed as fast as I could and went downstairs. In the kitchen, Cody and my mother were making waffles, oblivious to the danger my father was in, lost in a warm cocoon of oranges and vanilla and maple syrup. I grabbed my cherry-red jacket from the brass hooks in the foyer and slipped outside without even stopping to say good morning.

The streets were sheets of ice, shiny and smooth,

treacherous. I had to take baby steps the whole way and still I slipped every few feet. There was nothing to grab on to; ice covered everything. Finally, I reached Saint Sebastian's, the Catholic Church. Inside, there was a big crucifix with a suffering Jesus hanging from it and statues of saints in long robes, all with gold circles above their heads like someone's fancy china. I practically gasped. That's how beautiful it was in there.

I went straight up to the altar. The air smelled like wet wool and melting wax, a serious smell that I liked. I knelt down on the padded kneeler, clasped my hands, bent my head, and even though I thought you were probably supposed to whisper in church, I spoke in my natural speaking voice to be sure God heard me. "God, save my father from that avalanche." I just kept saying it, over and over. "God, save my father from that avalanche. God, save my father from that avalanche."

I was surprised how the whole time I was there, not one person came in. It was just me and God and Jesus on the cross and all of those saints. I said my prayer about a million times. That's what it was. A prayer. I couldn't imagine our life without my father. I mean, we were a family of four. And even though sometimes Cody drove me crazy, most of the time I liked the way we looked together, all of us. Maybe we didn't take ski vacations to fancy places and maybe our house needed a lot of work, but we were a great family. I didn't want to be just three. I didn't want my father to die and leave the rest of us alone. So I prayed. I prayed and I prayed and I prayed, pushing away the thoughts of what my life would be like without my father in it. Without him driving me to school and stopping at Seven Stars Bakery for hot chocolate and ginger scones. Without him teaching me new words or facts or songs. Without him taking my mother by the waist and spinning her around our kitchen floor while some old song played on the stereo.

I could tell by the way the light slanted differently through the stained glass windows that I had knelt and prayed for a long time. My throat felt raw, my voice was raspy, and I was burning hot. Outside, the ice had melted into fast rivulets of water that raced down the streets and sidewalks like it had somewhere to go. Still, it took me even longer to get home. My legs felt heavy and my head pounded. Maybe I was dying, I thought. Maybe I had suffered from hallucinations the night before. Maybe I had lost my mind.

But when I walked in the door, I knew immediately that everything had happened just as I had thought. There was panic in the air.

My mother emerged, red-eyed, from the kitchen, clutching Cody by the hand. Behind her, I saw Gran, my father's mother; and Aunt Birdie the cardiologist; and Aunt Becky the pediatrician; and other faces behind them, familiar and frightened.

"Madeline!" my mother said, and she started to cry. "Where in the world have you been?"

"Is Daddy dead?" I asked, my voice hoarse and sore.

"Why would you say that?" my mother asked. She was twisting a crumpled tissue in her hand. "Did you hear it on television last night after I went to bed?"

"Is he?" I said, and it came out all raspy.

Gran stepped forward, tall and erect, her silvery blond hair slightly droopier than usual.

"He's alive," she said. "We just got word that he's one of the people who made it."

I nodded.

"But how did you even know?" Mom asked, moving toward me. "How could you know?"

"Was it an avalanche?" I managed to whisper before I slumped to the floor in a sweaty, feverish heap.

From somewhere above me I heard my mother's voice, surprised, saying, "Yes."

I closed my eyes, smiling. I had done it. I had performed my second miracle, a huge miracle, a miraculous miracle.

"My God," someone said, "she's burning up!"

I felt myself being lifted and carried away, up, up, up. The next time I opened my eyes, it was night and still. My father was saved. And I was on my way to becoming a bona fide saint.

I didn't need to be a saint. I was already pretty busy. For one thing, there's my ballet, which is really important. I have blisters on my feet and a callus on my toe that is really gross. Also, I can do the most perfect arabesque. This requires great balance and fortitude. For another thing, I was working very hard on improving my vocabulary. I did all of the Word Power challenges in my grandparents' *Reader's Digest*s.

They kept them in the bathroom, and when the conversation got really boring I would go and sit in there and improve my vocabulary. They would always ask my mother if I had some kind of digestive issues. "Have you had Madeline's digestive tract checked recently?" they'd ask. And later, in the car on the way home, Mom would ask me, "What is it you do in there, Madeline?" But I couldn't answer her because I was reciting new words in my head: *turbulence, noun, disturbance of the atmosphere . . . jettison, verb, to cast off . . .*

Also, after my father came home, I wanted to spend as much time with him as possible. But, it seemed like something had changed. He looked gloomy and restless. Plus, he had to be in New York City all the time because his heli-skiing article was suddenly an article about surviving an avalanche and people were really really interested in it, and in him. After so many years of fluctuating incomes, his seemed to be only going up. But he acted miserable instead of happy.

Then one morning right after breakfast, my parents sat Cody and me down in the living room, a room we hardly ever sat in, and my mother wouldn't look at us. Instead, she kept staring at the pattern on the floor, her eyes tracing its edges. Dad looked right at us, though, and started to say things like someone on a television movie. "Sometimes people fall out of love," he said. And, "No one is to blame here." And, "I will always be your father and love you." I kept trying to get Mom to look at me. But she wouldn't.

Cody started to panic, "Do you mean you're getting divorced?"

I laughed. "Of course they're not getting divorced," I told him. Just the night before, we had made homemade pizza together and then we played Pictionary and then we all danced the chicken dance. Does that sound like a family about to get divorced?

I heard Dad say, "Yes. We are getting divorced."

Next thing I knew, he was telling us that we could visit him every other weekend in New York, and Cody shouted, "You're moving to New York?"

"He's not moving to New York, you dope," I said. It was like my brain couldn't process the information. I was hearing words, but they didn't seem to have any meaning.

Then Dad said, "I'm sorry. I really am." He looked sorry when he said that, but still, he kissed us both on the tops of our heads and walked out of the house into a new life.

All the while, Mom sat there staring at the floor. She never explained anything. She never tried to stop him from going. As soon as the door shut behind him, she ran to the window and watched him drive away. She was crying like crazy, and Cody was crying like crazy, and I said, "Do something, Mom! Do something!"

She finally turned and looked at me. In that one moment, she seemed to get a lot older. She looked at me and she said absolutely nothing. I think that's when I started to hate her.

"This is your fault," I said.

So how did I, Madeline Vandermeer, fairly normal girl from a fairly normal family, decide to become a saint? Well, when I saved my father's life, I somehow managed to ruin everything else. Now my life was all upside down, and frankly, I needed something to happen. If I performed just one more miracle, I believed I could fix everything and become a saint. The whole world would hear about me and the amazing things I'd done. I even wrote to the Pope at the Vatican in Rome, Italy, and asked him how to proceed. He probably understands about a hundred languages, even hard ones like Japanese, and remote ones like Swahili, and ancient ones that aren't even languages anymore. Certainly he can read English, an easy one, a popular one, the language of a future saint.

I told my mom that I wanted to be a saint and she said, "Madeline, we aren't even Catholic."

"That," I told her, "is a technicality."

The night I told my mother that I wanted to be a saint, she was making one of her disgusting dinners. She has a column for *Family* magazine and she writes recipes and stupid essays, every month. Why are they so stupid? Because we are not a family. We are three people—her and me and Cody—all living under the same leaky roof. A family likes one another. A family turns off all of the lights and stands in front of the big window and gazes down at the Statue of Liberty, each one of them holding their own breath at how magnificent she is, the way we do in my dad's New York City loft, with his new wife, Ava, and their baby.

"No, Madeline," Mom said, "it is not a technicality. It

is a requirement." She didn't even look at me. She just kept stirring and measuring. These are the kinds of things she does that drive me crazy.

I peered into the pot. Whatever was inside was far too green for me. I don't even like when they put parsley on my plate in restaurants.

"Did you know that some saints lived on nothing but air?" I asked Mom.

"That," she said, "is ridiculous."

To indicate that this conversation was over, she turned on her Cuisinart, which sounded like a helicopter landing in our kitchen.

"If you want to do something useful," I shouted, "why don't you invent a silent Cuisinart so that American families can converse while they cook?"

"What, Madeline?" Mom shouted back, pointing at her ears. "I can't hear you!"

And that, in a nutshell, was my problem. No one could hear me, except, I guess, God. But when I was an official saint, everyone would listen to what I had to say. My name would be in newspapers. I would be on television. A sculptor would come to our house and make a statue of me wearing long flowing robes and a gentle expression, maybe with a baby lamb or kitten at my feet. Biographers would write my life story for the history books. People would hang out on Lloyd Avenue in front of our house, waiting for a glimpse of me. I wouldn't have to go to school anymore, though I wasn't sure of all the rules and benefits of sainthood. The Pope would have to fill me in.

One thing I thought was that when I was a saint, I would probably have to forgive my mother for letting my father leave us. Saints are nice like that. Besides, before he left, I thought she was great. She did things like put faces on my hamburger buns. She would take those green olives with the red insides that come in a bottle and cut them in half and use those for the eyes, and a small round of sweet pickle for the nose and then a big red ketchup smile. Also, we used to cut shapes out of pieces of American cheese with cookie cutters so that my sandwiches always were one piece of white bread topped with a star, or a heart, or a moon.

When I remember things like this, I feel all weird. But then I look at my mother with her plain hair and her plain face and sad eyes and I get angry at her all over again. She let my dad leave us. Still, I keep trying for a third miracle. If I live as long as Mother Teresa did, I could perform something like a thousand miracles! Who knows? Maybe I can even perform a miracle that will fix everything. Saints do things like that, every day.

Chapter Two

THE TRIP OF A LIFETIME

AFTER MY PARENTS GOT DIVORCED and the very thing I worried about — life without my father — had happened, I missed our old life in Boston even more than before. So every Saturday after ballet class, I begged my mother to drive past our old apartment in Back Bay. Sometimes she would even do it. But usually she would sigh and say, "It's time to move on, Madeline." I had three best friends when we lived in Boston. They all had flower names: Poppy, Marigold, and Rose. This was just a coincidence. I really missed them. We used to take museum classes together every Saturday morning and meet in the playground near Poppy's apartment in the South End on beautiful afternoons. Then I moved and they just stayed their own happy bouquet.

Of course we pinky-swore that we would always always stay in touch and that they would come to Providence some weekend and I would visit them after ballet class sometimes but somehow, even though we were only an hour apart, none of those things really happened. Once, my mother arranged for me to call them. Poppy's mother gathered all three of them at their apartment and put them on speakerphone but no one talked. Not even me. Another time, we met Marigold and her mother for lunch after ballet, but my mother cried and talked about her divorce and Marigold and I stared at each other. She had on lip gloss. And Uggs.

This particular Saturday my mother was especially cranky but I asked, anyway. "Can we drive past our old apartment? Please, please, please?"

"I thought we'd go for tea at the Ritz-Carlton," she said.

Tea at the Ritz-Carlton was expensive. Something seemed very suspicious. "Okay," I said, knowing it wasn't okay. Then I thought of something. "Is Rose going to be there?" Rose had her tenth birthday party there, a real tea party, and we got all dressed up in pretty dresses and even got manicures.

"Rose?" my mother said, as if she had already forgotten who Rose even was. "Oh," she said. "No." Then she added all special-like, "Just us." But that made me feel bad because that's how I thought of our family without my father in it: just us.

We drove through the streets of beautiful Boston and I tried to memorize all the buildings, like the old State House, so that when I got home I could play them back in my mind.

"They moved," my mother said suddenly.

"Who?"

"The Palmers. Rose's family. They moved to Cleveland. We got a card at Christmas."

Then I got really mad because she hadn't even bothered to tell me. "Cleveland?" I said. If it wasn't a state capital, I didn't necessarily know which state something was in.

"Cleveland. Ohio," she said.

"Capital, Columbus," I said, satisfied. I wondered how Poppy and Marigold were managing now, and smiled, relieved,

I guess, that someone else in the world might be unhappy like me.

My mother was pulling up in front of the Ritz-Carlton, and letting the valet take our car. This was all feeling like a celebration, but my mother looked really glum. Her jaw was set kind of weird and she kept avoiding eye contact with me. Always a bad sign. Inside, we sat in the beautiful dining room and the waiters in their tuxedos treated us like movie stars. It was the first time I'd ever been there when they didn't bring me a coloring book and crayons, which meant I looked mature and sophisticated. Ballerinas can extend their necks and hold their chins just so for effect. I did this, imagining Madame instructing me: "Reach, Madeline. Reach!"

"What's wrong with your neck?" my mother said.

She really didn't know anything about anything. I wondered how, just a few short months ago, I used to think she was smart. Outside the window was the Boston Common and the Public Gardens, and I looked at them instead of her, stretching my neck. Reaching, reaching.

"Did you twist it or something in class?" she said, and I chose to ignore her.

I ordered Lapsang tea because the name was lyrical (new vocabulary word, number 100), and I filled my plate with all the miniature cakes and things, but my mother, who ordered Earl Grey, the most boring tea ever, just sat there.

When my mouth was full of scone, she said, "Well, Madeline, the thing is . . ."

Then she stopped talking and I stopped chewing and then she said, "Have you ever heard of the Providence Ballet Company? The ones who do *The Nutcracker* every year in Providence? In a college auditorium?"

I kept chewing, worried.

"Well," she said, "actually, I spoke to the teacher you would have there, Misty Glenn? And she said that they might be able to use a real theater this year."

"The teacher I would have?" I said. My scone had turned all dry in my mouth and I considered spitting it out. But you just don't spit out scones at the Ritz-Carlton. It isn't ballerina-like. It isn't even saintlike.

"Oh, Madeline," she said, and her face crumpled the way it did right before she started to cry. "I just can't do it anymore."

"Do what?" I said. I glanced around to make sure no one was watching her. But the room was full of a bunch of old ladies in wool suits and gray buns, sipping and staring at nothing at all.

"Ever since your father left, I am having organizational problems," she said. She made a weird face, trying not to cry.

"Okay," I said.

"This drive into Boston every Saturday is too much. The traffic, the time, finding someone to watch Cody, Cody crying because he doesn't want me to leave him, the cost of this class over one that's literally right down the street from home —"

My face didn't crumple. I didn't twist it all funny. I just cried. Hard. My mother had already driven my father away, and now she was taking the one thing that mattered the most in the world to me. Maybe God was testing me or something. Aren't saints supposed to be tested? But this was too much. She was telling me how I would be in the advanced class with Misty Glenn. She was telling me that soon they were having auditions for a ballet set to Vivaldi's *Four Seasons* and

I could try out. But all I could do was sit there and cry and hate her even more.

Then, the next week, she gave me more bad news.

"It's going to be the trip of a lifetime," my mother said. Of course I didn't believe her. She was an expert on exactly nothing. Unless you counted messing up lives. *That* she was excellent at. For starters, I now took ballet lessons with a woman who looked like a cheerleader and chewed gum while she showed us what to do. Also, her cell phone always rang during class and her ring tone was the theme from *The Addams Family* TV show.

I watched my mother lay a bunch of maps and guidebooks on the kitchen table.

"Naples," she said, opening one of the books to a picture of happy people eating pizza at an outdoor café. "Florence," she said, opening a different book and pointing to an enormous statue of a naked man. "This," she said, "is Michelangelo's *David*."

"Who cares?" I said, and made myself yawn.

"Imagine it," she said. "Pompeii! Pizza! Italy! I can't say enough about Italy!"

My mother has the plainest face in the world. Her eyes are brown, her hair is brown. All ordinary. She likes to remind me that when I was little I thought she was the most beautiful woman in the world. Last time she said that, I told her, "Oh, really? Well, I also thought Mount Rushmore got that way naturally. So I guess I made a lot of mistakes." This was called a *zinger*, and Sophie and I practiced them sometimes after school if she had nothing better to do. Zingers are mean. Lately, sometimes I get a strong urge to be mean to my mother.

"What do you think?" she said now in her best upbeat voice.

"I think you should wear lipstick every day," I said. That was not a zinger. That was sarcasm, which is even harder.

"Thank you for the beauty advice, Madeline," she said. She didn't sound upbeat anymore. I smiled at her and she smiled back, both of us sarcastic. "Now tell me what you think about our trip to Italy."

I said, "I don't want to go."

Outside, it was still winter, a rainy gray winter. The streets of Providence were like an obstacle course of puddles and slush and old snow that had gone dirty and hard.

"Of course you want to go to Italy," my mother said. "Everybody wants to go to Italy. It's something people want."

"Well, I want to go to New York City and spend the summer with Daddy. *He* said he'll take me to the ballet. *He* said he'll take me to Queens where there's a painting of a saint that weeps. Real tears," I added because I could read my mother's mind and knew she was thinking it was a hoax.

Then, to be good and rude, I opened up the book *The Song of Bernadette* about how a peasant girl in France saw the Virgin Mary and got all of these orders from her, like to build a church in a particular place and have sick people come and bathe in water from the spring. Bernadette became a saint. I was keeping a list of what I had in common with other saints, and number one on my list was that I was a peasant, too. It looked like rich people never got to be saints, so that eliminated Sophie.

"Besides," I said to my mother, "I thought we didn't have any money. I thought we were peasants. How can a bunch of peasants afford to go to Italy?" We had read about peasants in school, too. Peasants tilled the land, we learned. They were poor, but they were good, hardworking people.

"Peasants!" my mother shrieked.

"Peasants helped people," I told her. "In World War Two. It's nothing to be embarrassed about."

"What has gotten into you?" she mumbled under her breath.

I knew what she was thinking. She talked about it with Mrs. Harrison all the time.

They were embarrassing, those talks. And she and Mrs. Harrison had them right in front of me, as if I were invisible. "It's those teen years I read about when she was tiny," my mother said. "They seemed so far away, so unlikely then." Just yesterday, when Mrs. Harrison came to pick me up for school and I refused to wear the silly, bright yellow slicker and matching boots my mother had bought me as if I were a baby duckling instead of a twelve-year-old — a miracle worker, a soon-to-be saint — she shouted from the porch to Mrs. Harrison, "She still wears flowered underpants but *these* are too babyish." So now the whole world knows about my underpants. Mrs. Harrison gave my mother a big sympathetic look. Then when I got in her ridiculously humongous SUV she said, "Madeline, why can't you try to help your mother?"

I watched over the top of *The Song of Bernadette* while my mother sat staring at all her stupid books and maps. My father never uses guidebooks. He just goes places. He explores. He has adventures. Even in the days when they were married and supposedly happy, they would argue over traveling techniques, my mother reading from a guidebook and my father ignoring her.

"Trust me on this, Madeline," she said suddenly, brightly, in a way that made me immediately suspicious. "You are going to love this trip. We'll go to Italy and you can go to churches where there are saints' actual bodies right there."

"Like who?" I said.

"Saint Agatha," my mother said.

"Saint Agatha?"

"Only thirteen years old and the emperor made her stand naked in public because she rejected some guy's advances. So she's standing there naked and miraculously her hair starts to grow. And it grows and grows until it covers her nakedness completely."

I considered this.

"Well," I said, turning back to my book. "That might be interesting."

What else might be interesting came to me then, too. If I went to Rome, then I could go talk to the Pope. I didn't want to sound too excited so I said, "I'll think about it."

"Oh, yes," my mother said, oh so smug, "there are so many saints in Italy. Catherine of Siena, Saint Claire, Saint Francis, Saint —"

"I get it, okay?" I said. But I was, I admit, tingling with excitement.

Of course, divorce changes a lot of things. For example, all of the stuff I was worried about while I prayed in church the day of the avalanche wound up happening anyway. My dad was okay, but no more ginger scones on the way to school. No more slow dancing in the kitchen. In Humanities class we learned about point of view. This is the way a writer tells a story. A point of view is very specific, and changes the way the character sees the world. Well, from my point of view my mother kept getting worse and worse. It wasn't just the way she cried all the time, or made stupid decisions, or lost things, or even the way she stopped looking pretty. But she started to seem foolish. Her job seemed foolish. Her hair seemed foolish. The things she said seemed foolish. From my point of view, my mother was foolish.

Once, a few months after my father moved out, I found a list she had made. She was seeing a therapist with the unbelievable name of Doctor Sane. Doctor Sane always had her do things like draw animals to represent her emotions and make memory boxes and other completely idiotic tasks. This one, written in my mother's excellent penmanship instead of on the computer, said at the top:

The good things in my life:

1. The kids, of course.
2. The house. Its wainscoting in every room. Its claw-foot tubs. The butler's bell that still works. The only slightly chipped stained glass window in the front foyer. The maze of crooked stairs and multiple stairways that lead to each floor. The nicotiana that blooms beside the front porch and fills the evening air with its sweet smell. My bookshelf-lined office. The screened-in porch that inexplicably juts from that office, even though it's on the second floor. The house is the kind of house I imagined myself in as a child growing up

in a split ranch in Indiana. Of course, I also imagined a husband but I won't go there.

3. My monthly column "Food Is Fun!" in <u>Family</u>. My job is to create recipes that are healthy, interesting, and delicious. Nothing like creamed canned tuna on toast like my own mother used to make. Instead, I write about things like fun Asian food — cold noodles with peanut butter sauce, steamed dumplings, wilted bok choy. The kids hate this food I make for the column. They want what they call "real food" — macaroni and cheese from a box, chicken nuggets, fish sticks. Still, every Friday night, after a week of researching ideas and writing my column, we all sit down together and test my recipes. They grimace and gag and spit out my carefully rolled turkey meatballs, my tortellini with a creamy artichoke heart sauce, my delicate flan. "Kids love cream sauce," I write later that night, after my own kids have gorged themselves on nacho cheese tortilla chips and gone to bed. "And they will take to artichoke hearts the way our generation took to SpaghettiO's."

I like this column because I get to be creative, for one thing, and because I get to bring in $2500 a month, which makes me feel independent from my no-good, suddenly incredibly wealthy, married to somebody else husband. I mean ex-husband. But I won't go there.

4. My cookbook, _Cooking for Kids Is Fun!_. It sold moderately well in big cities like Boston and Los Angeles and failed miserably in places like my own home state of Indiana. The book is filled with sidebars about things like the joys of berry picking with your kids, then going home and making fresh jams and cobblers. On the back cover is a black-and-white picture of me grinning foolishly, with a somber Cody on one side of me and a scowling Madeline on the other, standing in front of our 1919 enamel Glenwood stove, looking like we were straight out of _Little House on the Prairie_. Did I mention that I also love that stove?

5. (or is it 6?) _Family_ is sending me to Italy to research authentic Italian recipes. When I get back, I get to write a feature called "Traveling With Kids Is Fun!" My editor, Jessica, a single, childless woman in her twenties, is delighted by even the moderate success of the cookbook. "I've got big plans for you," Jessica said, and on my good days I imagine summers in Asia, in South America, in India. I imagine more cookbooks, a wider audience. I imagine myself

as famous as that wonderful ex-husband of mine, Scott, as rich as Scott. That's on my good days. Did I mention that I don't like Jessica? She is fifteen years younger than I am, a real blonde, a Harvard graduate. She dates an MTV talk show host. She wears short dresses and knee-high suede boots in colors like lavender and baby blue. Jessica is a hard person to like.

7. (or is it 6? There is no 7 (or is it 6?))

I took that list and folded it very small, the way I folded notes in school that were not meant for just anybody to read. It proved things, this list. It proved that my mother did not like Jessica even though whenever she talked to her on the phone she gushed and said things like, "You are something else!" It proved my mother was crazy jealous of my father, just because he was brave and smart and had done something meaningful with his life, unlike her. It proved how insincere and insecure she was. How could a person like my mother keep a person like my father in love with her? If she had been different, someone more like his new wife, Ava, we would still be a family. The list proved everything.

* * *

On the way to school the morning after our mother gave us the thrilling news about the trip to Italy, Cody made an announcement: He was afraid. He was afraid of Mount Vesuvius erupting and then burning us to death while we were in Italy. But I knew, and even our mother knew, that he was also afraid of swimming in the ocean because there could be sharks; of sailing because there could be icebergs; of sleeping alone because there were ghosts, vampires, strangers; of flying because planes crashed or, worse, disappeared into the Bermuda Triangle. Cody was probably the only five-year-old kid who preferred the History Channel over Nickelodeon.

Mom put on her most cheerful voice.

"We probably won't even see Mount Vesuvius, buddy," she said, glancing into the rearview mirror at Cody, who sat stiffly smack in the middle of the backseat.

"That's all you see in Naples," I said.

"Why, thank you, Madeline, for your sudden interest in the geography of Italy," my mother said, glaring.

I sat beside Cody, squashed between the door and his car seat. Would he ever outgrow that stupid thing? I wondered, scowling over my Spanish vocabulary words. My father said

Spanish was perhaps the single most important thing I would learn because one day soon more people would speak Spanish than any other language. My father was always right.

"We don't have airbags, do we?" Cody said anxiously.

"In this old heap?" I laughed. "You've got to be kidding!" Mom drove an embarrassing 1984 Volvo 240 with almost two hundred thousand miles on it and a huge dent on the front from the time she chased after my father once when they were fighting. She plowed right into Sophie's parents' new Lexus. "Now look what you've done," my father said, jumping out of his own VW.

"They didn't even have airbags when they made this car," I told Cody. "They weren't even invented yet."

"Because airbags kill kids, right?" Cody said, looking at me.

"Volvos are the safest cars made," Mom said. "Did you know that?"

"You told me a zillion times," he said, sighing.

"There you go," she said, forcing a smile.

"Miles's mother has airbags in her car. So don't let her ever pick me up, okay?"

"Gotcha," she said. "Right-o." She took a breath.

Miles's mother was supposed to pick Cody up from school that very afternoon. It was written on the big calendar in the kitchen. I started to keep count of my mother's lies. Two since we got in the car and the entire day still stretched before us. Sometimes my mother tells me that I have an unbalanced view of what has happened to our family. "There are two sides to every story, Madeline," she likes to say. But my father doesn't lie. In his kind of journalism, he *exposes* lies.

"First grade is the hardest grade, right?" Cody said. "I'm in the hardest grade right now, right?"

"Oh, please," I groaned. "Do you have Spanish? Do you have to know the state capitals? All fifty of them?"

"So," Mom said, "about my great news. The trip? Isn't it great? You and me and Madeline. The three of us. All together." She looked at me in the mirror and added, "All expenses paid. By the magazine."

That was how peasants went to Italy, I suppose.

"I don't want to go," Cody said. "I want to stay home with you and watch television this summer. I want first grade to be done for me and you to stay in bed all day and watch —"

"Italy!" our mother said with so much enthusiasm that

she swerved the car into the next lane. "We're all going to Italy and we'll see museums and the Colosseum. We'll see everything."

She glanced back again. Cody had slumped down so far I wondered if she could see him at all.

"You can pick the things you want to see and we'll go see them," she said weakly.

"Uh-huh," said Cody.

"Great," she said. "Isn't this great?"

"Uh-huh."

"Clearly," I said, closing my Spanish book firmly, "we are both sooooo thrilled."

We turned into the school parking lot, where kids were pulling out of minivans and station wagons. They all seemed so much happier than us, practically skipping through puddles in their bright rain boots, flashes of red and yellow and green, backpacks swaying as they moved. I looked down at my own stupid shoes, imagining my bright yellow rain boots left behind in the front hallway. When had bright rain boots become cool? And how did my mom know? Why did these things always pass me by?

"Here we are," our mother said, turning off the car.

"Uh-huh," Cody said.

She sat there for an instant, then she said, "You know, you two, I wish I could twitch my nose and make your lives better — put Cody in the top reading group, beatify Madeline, give you both a full-time father, one who wouldn't leave."

She was about to cry; I knew that. This was the very type of thing she said before she started to cry. So I chose not to correct her and tell her that saints got canonized, not beatified.

I saw the smiling face of Miles's mother, Julia, hooded in a bright green rain slicker. Then she tapped on the window and my mother sniffled and took deep, relaxing breaths, which is what she did to pull herself together. The window on the driver's side no longer went down (or if it went down it did not go back up); so my mother opened my window instead. Everything about Julia was bigger than life: hair, face, fingernails. She was like a Godzilla, and by that I mean the original Godzilla, not the terrible remake. "Remakes stink!" my father always said.

Julia leaned her big head in and grinned at Cody. "Hey!"

she said in her Southern drawl. "You're coming home with me today, you little goober."

I winced, right in her face. Julia called all children "goober," which she claimed meant "peanut." "Trust me," Julia would say, "I'm from Georgia and I know my peanuts." But it reminded me of something in your nose. Privately, Cody and I called Julia "booger," which always sent Cody into a fit of giggles.

Beside us loomed Julia's car, also big, and brand-new, with airbags waiting to get Cody.

Julia opened the back door and I jumped out. She was already adjusting Cody's backpack, tightening the straps even though he liked them so loose that the pack bounced against him. Miles and his older sister Suki were waiting patiently at the front door of school, frozen in place like kids in a J. Crew catalogue. I stood next to my mother and watched as Cody let himself be led away by Julia. His backpack was my old one from kindergarten, purple with hot pink trim. He wore my old rain slicker, too, a yellow one with a hood made like a duck's face, the bill an orange visor, two eyes peering above it. The combination made him look small and vulnerable, like a kid that anything could happen to. Mom must have been thinking the same thing because she called out to him.

"Cody!" she called. "You'll be in the back. Don't worry."

Julia and Cody turned. "What's that?"

"The airbags," Mom shouted, "are only in the front!"

Julia looked at her, confused, but Cody nodded.

"Have a good day!" our mother shouted to him.

"You, too!" he said, his voice tiny and high.

I thought maybe Mom should have walked him inside, but she was already upset so I didn't point that out to her.

Cody's voice drifted across the parking lot to us.

"What?" Mom shouted.

"I said," he screamed, "in a plane crash do the kids die, too? Or just the grown-ups?"

"The plane won't crash, Cody!" Mom called to him. "It's going to be great! You'll see!" But Cody didn't wait for her to answer. He just kept walking fast with his head down.

Señor Valdez, my Spanish teacher, stopped to stare at us from under his umbrella. I pretended not to notice. Finally, right before I died from embarrassment, he started walking again. I jumped out of the car, fast.

"Oh, yeah," I said, hurrying away from my mother, "we're all just fine."

One of my favorite things to do was listen in on my parents' telephone conversations. Even before they got divorced I liked doing it. Back then it was stuff like "Can you pick up Madeline at ballet?" or "Can you call Alexis to babysit?" Stuff that made me feel like warm toast inside. Family stuff. We don't have a family now. It's more like an unraveled sweater, pieces of it everywhere, the whole thing coming apart. The whole thing ugly. More irony: My mother worked for *Family* magazine. Ha!

I used to pick up the phone and listen and not even care if they knew. "Hang up, Madeline," Mom might say. Or Dad would say, "What are we going to do about Mad? Send her to spy school?" in a really deep fake voice and then I would laugh. And then we would all three laugh. But once they got divorced I had to be more careful because chances were they would be fighting when I picked up the phone. If my mother was downstairs on the kitchen phone, I had to slip into her office and switch the phone on to speaker. They never knew I was sitting there listening.

After the trip of a lifetime got announced, they had a lot of long-distance arguments.

"I think it would have been good, appropriate even, if you had asked me before deciding to take my kids halfway around the world," my father said.

"Really?" my mother said. "Well, I think it would have been good, appropriate even, if you'd asked before you decided to leave our family."

My mother spent that first year crying and angry. Angry that he'd left her, angrier that he'd married someone else. *That tart,* she used to say. That was my mother's idea of a joke; he had married a woman who made tarts for a living, the woman gourmet magazines called *The Tart Lady, Ava Pomme.* My mother did not even believe that her real name was Ava Pomme, that someone who would grow up to make tarts for a living would be named the equivalent of *apple,* and that her most famous tart was in fact her apple tart. "It's all a little too convenient, isn't it?" my mother wondered out loud all too often.

"Actually," my father continued, "I don't think you can even take them without my permission."

"Scott," she said, "don't be foolish. The magazine is paying for me to take the kids and eat our way through Italy. It's a once-in-a-lifetime opportunity."

My mother had this idea about my father's new life, that it was filled with champagne and perfectly flaky crust, with a country house and a loft in the city, with cocktail parties and black-tie events. For the most part, she was right. What made her feel even worse was that in just one year, my father and Ava were married with a baby of their own, a little girl named Zoe. They were a family. They were a family and *we weren't*. We were three people who lived unhappily in a run-down house in Providence. I wanted to be a part of my father's real family more than anything, except being a saint. If I wasted my time making lists, number one, I would be a saint, number two I would live in New York City in my father's real family, and number three, I would be in a full-time ballet school.

Another bad habit of my mother's was to tell and retell the same old story to anyone who would listen. Mrs. Harrison had probably heard it all a million times by now, how the winter before the divorce my father went to Idaho on an assignment about helicopter skiing. They had just bought the house, and the article would earn them enough money to pay for the renovations. The avalanche happened and everyone except Dad and a dentist from Chicago was killed. My father turned his article into a bestselling book called *Avalanche: Skiing Toward Disaster*, moved to New York City, married Ava Pomme, and had a new baby.

For a while, we couldn't even turn on the television without seeing Dad and Ava. He told his harrowing tale on the *Today* show and *Oprah*, and Ava stood teary-eyed and lovingly beside him. "As if she had been the one waiting for the calls from the Sun Valley Hospital to see if he was all right," my mother said in the same old story. "As if she was the one who waited for him at Logan Airport when he returned, the one who stayed up with him at night, waiting for him to talk about what he had lived through." Oprah had turned her moist eyes on Ava and said, right on national television, "This must be so hard for you to hear," and Ava Pomme, the Tart Lady, had nodded, had dabbed at her eyes with a linen handkerchief, had put her hand over his — "Possessively!" my mother added dramatically, pathetically, endlessly — while we all sat, miserable and abandoned, in our unrenovated house.

The thing is, while we watched him on television last year, we were all miserable for separate reasons. I liked seeing my father on famous television shows with a glamorous woman and I felt miserable that instead of waiting in the Green Room with movie stars I was sitting with a mother who screamed and threw shoes and Legos at the TV set. I asked Dad if I could go with him when he taped one of these shows, but he said my mother needed me more.

By the time the trip of a lifetime negotiations began, Zoe was born and a whole year had gone by. Even though he wasn't on TV so much anymore, his cell phone was always ringing and he was always e-mailing editors from his BlackBerry. He was famous. He was in demand. And even though I missed him like crazy, from my point of view, my father was anything but foolish.

I almost forgot I was listening in on their phone conversation. Then I heard my father saying, "First of all, Madeline doesn't even want to go."

"You mean second of all," Mom said.

"What?"

"First of all was I hadn't asked your permission," she said. "Second of all, Madeline doesn't want to go. And I can save you third of all because Cody doesn't want to go, either."

"So you go and the kids will spend the summer here with us."

I held my breath. It was only three in the afternoon, but already the sky was dark, threatening still more of the cold rain that had marked most of January. In New York City, gray skies looked romantic. Here, they only looked dull.

"You know," Mom said, "I started to build a playhouse for the kids last fall. I thought I could finish it, but it was harder than I expected. I had to keep redoing it."

"Alice," Dad said, and I could hear the dread in his voice. My mother could very quickly deteriorate into an ex-wife from soap operas, all tears and accusations. "Don't."

"What I am trying to say is, I make plans and I work on them until I get them right."

"Okay," he said carefully.

"And I'm planning this trip and we're all going. All three of us. You can see them before and you can see them after. But for one month this summer those kids are mine."

Silence. Silence for so long that I had to check to make

sure we were all still connected. We were. New York City in summer, I knew, was hot and humid and the subway smelled like pee. But I didn't care. When you are part of a family, things like that don't really matter. Just when I started imagining it, how I could forget about my mother and Cody and disappear into my father's family, into New York City, my father spoke. His voice cutting into my daydream startled me so much, I almost screamed.

"This is an ongoing dialogue," he said. "The trip, the details, all of it."

"We leave June twentieth," my mother said, and let the date sit there between them, stretching across Connecticut right into my father's loft in Tribeca. She waited, then said in a dewy voice, a voice I'd come to hate because it was supposed to make everybody pity her, "I guess that date doesn't mean a thing to you anymore."

June twentieth would have been their fifteenth wedding anniversary. *I* still remembered that date, so I knew he had to remember it, too, the way my mother would get all dressed up fancy and spray on too much Chanel Number 5. She'd wear lipstick, too, and mascara. Ava Pomme wore those things all the time, but my mother never did. Except on their anniversary. She'd let me take a pair of new stockings out of the funny silver plastic egg they came in and unroll them for her. We'd wait by the door for my father to come in and act like he'd forgotten. "Oh," he'd say, "is dinner formal tonight?" Until finally he'd produce a dozen long-stem roses and they would kiss all romantic like two people in love.

My throat started to get funny. It's weird when your parents aren't in love anymore. It doesn't make sense. "It's complicated," both of them say whenever I ask them about this. For my whole life, until the divorce, almost nothing was complicated. Now everything was.

"Does it mean anything, Scott?" Mom asked, her voice all soft.

Some teeny part of me thought that maybe that question would change everything. Of course Dad remembered that he was the guy in that wedding picture with Mom, the one with the goofy grin on his face and the slightly crooked bow tie. He was the one who wrote their wedding vows and had them printed all fancy and framed. He was the one who hung those vows in their bedroom, right above their bed.

I wanted to yell into the phone, "Of course you remember, Dad!"

But instead, I turned off the speakerphone. I didn't want to hear his answer. In some ways, even though I hated to admit it, my mother and I were actually a lot alike.

Chapter Three

AVA POMME, THE TART LADY

"When people die," Cody said, "they disappear."

Our mother concentrated on her own reflection in the mirror, putting on a color of lipstick called Walnut Stain. It sounded like something you used on a piece of furniture getting refinished. She'd dragged us to Nordstrom earlier, where we had to watch her wander around in the makeup department like a zombie. She did fine at the local supermarket. But put her in a place where they sold something other than food and she couldn't handle it.

"But when they faint," Cody continued, "they only half disappear."

"Not exactly," she said.

She put her finger in her mouth, puckered her lips, then pulled her finger out of the tight *O* of her mouth. This is how you kept lipstick from getting on your teeth, she had explained to me after the woman at Nordstrom had explained it to her. I filed that away for future use.

As if he hadn't heard her, Cody said, "But what happens when a person gets divorced? They're not exactly disappeared, but you can't exactly see them, either."

"Don't stand on the tub," she said, frowning.

"When a person gets divorced," Cody said, "do they get like sort of frozen?"

Our mother turned around and lifted him off the edge of the tub, where he stood gripping the shower curtain, an old plastic thing covered with black-and-white images of movie stars from the 1940s. Joan Crawford and Katherine Hepburn and Jimmy Stewart. Our father had picked it out. We used to watch *Classic Theater* every Friday night on Channel 36. This was before Cody was born. The three of us used to scrunch together on our old sofa, the one the color of eggplants, and share a bowl of popcorn that Dad had made on the stove, not in the microwave, with freshly grated parmesan cheese on top. He could name any movie and who starred in it without even thinking very hard. On the other hand, our mother always got Brad Pitt and Leonardo DiCaprio mixed up. Never mind *old* movie stars.

"Tomorrow we're getting a new shower curtain," she mumbled, more to herself than to Cody, who now stood before her, gazing up into her face.

"No!" he said, horrified. "I love this one! It has all these people's faces on it. This lady and this guy," he added, jabbing at Bette Davis and Humphrey Bogart. Poor Cody! By the time he was old enough to watch old black-and-white movies with us, there was no more us.

She kneeled down in front of Cody.

"I'm divorced and I haven't disappeared, have I?" she said softly.

He frowned, trying unsuccessfully to wrap a piece of her hair around his finger. He used to fall asleep that way, curling a strand of her hair around his finger and tugging on it gently. But after the divorce Mom had cut her hair shorter and shorter, first in a chin-length bob, then having the back as short as a boy's but with the front still long enough to tuck behind her ears, and now all of it in short layers. I hated it. She didn't even look like herself anymore.

"You haven't disappeared but like right now you're going away," Cody said.

"Not away," she corrected. "Just out. For a few hours."

"With a man who isn't Daddy because Daddy is in New York, frozen."

"That's so stupid," I said, breaking my own ten-minute-old decision to not talk to either of these people. "Do you really think that Daddy just sits around while we're here? He has a life, you know."

Even as I said it, I was wondering if my father and Ava and Baby Zoe were scrunched together on their couch watching old movies and eating popcorn made on top of the stove and sprinkled with parmesan cheese.

"He's busy with his assignments," I said, because I had to say something or else I might start to cry. I didn't like thinking about Dad doing all those family things without me. "He's flying around the world and writing about important things that really matter to the planet — and humanity."

I glanced at my mother. Surely even she knew that column of hers was stupid, a waste of time to write and to read. Surely she knew that my father did something worthwhile with his lengthy articles about rain forest destruction and the commercialization of the environment. On my bedroom wall, nestled between a shrine to Saint Teresa and another to Mary Magdalene, my own patron saint, I hung the cover of the Sunday *New York Times Magazine* with his article about the death of Yellowstone from over-tourism, framed and even autographed. The father of a saint should be doing good for the world.

"Oh, yeah?" Cody said, close to tears. "Well, I think what he writes about is stupid and I wish he had disappeared in that dumb avalanche. I really do."

"Oh, honey, I know you're mad at him but you don't wish that. You love Daddy," Mom said.

"No, I don't!" Cody yelled, and he ran from the bathroom and up the stairs, slamming his bedroom door loud.

"I hope you're happy now, Madeline," my mother said, following Cody.

"Have a nice date," I said, in a fake sweet voice.

Her date was a man who made expensive drinking glasses.

A glass sculptor, he called himself. His name was Jamie and he had silver hair that was way too long, hanging almost to his collarbone in dramatic waves. It was their third date. To me, his glasses looked warped, the way the windows on our house looked. They were rimmed in vivid colors and sat on different colored stems. On their first date, he had brought my mother two champagne glasses; one was deep orange and ruby, the other emerald green and cerulean. That's what *he* called the colors. To me, they seemed like ordinary colors.

"The idea of it! Melting glass!" my mother had gushed, grinning all stupid while I thought about how ugly those glasses were. "Once," she had babbled, "my ex-husband and I visited the Big Island of Hawaii and hiked through Volcano National Park to watch hot lava flow out of the volcano and into the ocean below. Of course, I realize now that one of the things fundamentally wrong with our marriage was that Scott enjoys such things: trekking in Nepal, rock climbing in the West, scuba diving, while I don't like any of it."

Even though it was true, I couldn't believe she was spilling all of this personal stuff before they'd even left the house. Although my mother could ski, she avoided expert trails and stuck to bunny slopes. She did not like to swim to points too distant from the shore or venture any place too high above the ground. Like Cody, she was afraid of most things. I had thought for sure this guy wouldn't stick around. But now they were going on their third date. Maybe he was even going to be my mother's boyfriend.

When Mom returned to the bathroom, I was practicing putting on mascara. Every time the wand came near my eyes, I blinked them shut or poked myself so that now I had eyes like a raccoon with black mascara circles around them. "Who could kiss a guy with long stupid hair like that?" I asked

"Do you have a comment about every single thing?" Mom said. She was doing something weird with her hair, plopping globs of wax on it and making it stick up all over her head. She looked like someone who had been electrocuted. Ava used rosemary mint shampoo that came in a bottle shaped like waves, not the cheapo drugstore kind. Ava did not look electrocuted.

"What are you doing?" I asked my mother, disgusted.

"I am trying to have a life!" she shrieked.

With her hair like that and her eyes bulging the way they did when she got mad, she looked crazy. So crazy that I laughed.

And as soon as I laughed, she started to cry.

"This is dysfunctional," I said. "I will be in therapy for the rest of my life!" Carolyn MacNamara from school went to therapy every Wednesday. She had dark circles under her eyes, pointy bones, and divorced parents.

I decided to stay in my room all night and write another letter to the Pope about my sainthood. Certainly someone who would put up with all of this all the time — a mother who wanted her hair to stand up like she'd been electrocuted, who laughed and cried without any reason, who shouted at her daughter — certainly all of these things would help my cause.

I was writing the letter when my father called. Of course, I listened in.

"It's fine, Alice," he was saying. "Take them to Italy."

"What?" Mom said.

"That's right," Dad said, "because I worked on getting an assignment in Rome and the *Times* just gave me the okay. This way I'll be there, too, and I can see my kids."

"Fine!" Mom said. "If you have to one-up me every single time —"

"Don't get paranoid," Dad said.

I hung up quick. They were about to have a big fight and I didn't want to hear. Besides, I was happy. Dad was going to be in Rome this summer. Italy was looking better and better.

One of the things my mother hated most about the divorce was putting us on that train to New York City once a month. She hated the way I always dressed in black for the trip to New York, how I pretended I actually lived in Manhattan and was on my way home instead of *away* from home. She hated the way that Cody always pressed his face to the window, distorting his features so that he appeared like something floating in a jar of formaldehyde. Until that phone rang five or six hours later, she was all nerves and jumpiness. I knew all this because she always told me, every single time.

But this time we were all boarding the train together. Cody and I were off to visit our father and Mom was on her way to a meeting and dinner with her editor, Jessica. She wore black, too: the pants she called Katherine Hepburn pants and a cashmere sweater, the one thing she'd splurged on for herself with her cookbook royalties. Her college roommate Melissa had told her that a girl needed something cashmere, the bigger the better. "Melissa knows these things," my mother told me. "That's dumb advice," I said, just to be contrary.

She had on her Walnut Stain lipstick and she'd waxed her hair again. I decided to sit alone.

"You can sit alone only if I can see you," my mother said.

So I took the seat in front of my mother and Cody.

"Isn't this fun?" I heard her ask Cody. He was going to practice writing his numbers. He always made his 3s and 6s backward, but very neat.

"It is, Mommy," he said. "I'm so glad you came with us. When you don't come, Madeline won't even talk to me. She just listens to her iPod and eats all the snacks."

I rolled my eyes, even though they couldn't see me. For one thing, I only had an old Shuffle to listen to. Everyone on the planet had iPods that played videos but I had this ancient thing. Also, I had no cell phone. Saints shouldn't be so materialistic, I guess, but Bernadette didn't have to keep up with technology.

"This time *we'll* eat all the snacks," my mother said, like that would bother me.

"Go ahead," I said, sticking my face against the crack between the seats. "I hate those stupid rice cakes you always pack and I hate that bread with the cream cheese."

"Good," my mother said, leaning toward the crack. I could smell her coffee breath. "You can go to the diner car and get whatever it is you do like."

"I want an Am on Rye," I said. When she didn't laugh, I said, "Get it? *Am* instead of ham because we're on Amtrak. And Rye because we go through Rye, New York."

"The pun," she said, "is the lowest form of humor."

She opened her book then. It was a mystery, set in England, her favorite thing to read. She always liked trying to solve the murder, and the foreign setting, which somehow made everything even more ominous and seemingly impossible to solve. She always used to tell me the plots of these novels and together we would try to figure out who the bad guy was. But lately, I'd lost interest.

"Want to know the setup?" she asked.

Even though a little part of me wanted to say yes, I leaned back in my seat and said, "No, thanks."

"It's a good one," she said.

I looked out the window at all the trees whizzing by. "I'm not in the mood," I said finally.

Her seat seemed to sigh as she settled herself into it for the four-hour ride to New York City and Dad.

At Penn Station, we made our way through a confusing stairway to the arrivals board where our father always met us. On the train, our mother had gone into the bathroom right before we arrived and put on some more lipstick and a big spray of Chanel Number 5. "For Jessica," she'd said. "I need to look professional."

After twenty minutes beneath the clattering arrivals board with no sign of my father, she asked me, "Is he always late like this?" When she asked things like that I always felt like she was keeping notes somewhere of every single thing he did or didn't do.

Cody said, "He's always standing right here when we come up the escalator. He always has flowers for Madeline and a new Brio train for me."

"What?" she said.

A few years ago, when she had wanted to get Cody a train

set for Christmas, our father had called it an extravagance and refused.

"So you have a train set at Daddy's?" she asked.

"Yeah. And it's got a drawbridge and two tunnels and about fifteen hundred trains," Cody said. "Where is Daddy, anyway?"

I was just about to strangle Cody when I saw the most beautiful sight: Ava Pomme. She was walking toward us, her hair shiny and her clothes perfect.

I waved like mad. "There's Ava!"

Our mother spun around to look.

"Why'd he send her?" Cody mumbled.

Ava and our mother had never actually met. This was the first time I'd seen them side by side like this. Ava was a good five inches taller, with long rich brown hair falling over the collar of an oversize, below-the-knee camel cashmere coat, the sight of which made me embarrassed by my mother, standing there in her meager Old Navy pea coat. Ava wore black cigarette pants and boots with heels that my mother couldn't walk on to save her life. She wore stupid shoes that she bought in Chinatown — fat black things with a strap across the instep. My mother looked short and dumpy. As

Ava got closer, she reached out her hand, her legs so long and thin that all I could think of were deer running through meadows. My mother was more like a chipmunk.

"It's a real pleasure," Ava was saying.

"Where's Daddy?" Cody demanded.

"His plane is late," she said with a shrug. "He's coming in from Chile and he has sweaters for all of us."

She said *Chee-lay* as if Spanish were her true language. I practically swooned.

"Oh, goodie," my mother said sarcastically. "Even me?"

Ava laughed. "Maybe. You can never tell what Scott might do. So," Ava said to me, "let's get going, shall we? Marthe has the baby and I promised we'd come right back." She turned her attention back to Mom. "Marthe's our nanny. Honestly, she runs our life. We wouldn't be able to get out of bed in the morning without her."

I adored Marthe, even though I never understood anything she was saying. She smelled like sweet cinnamon buns, the kind my mother used to make for breakfast on snowy mornings. I missed those mornings, Mom and Dad bustling around the kitchen and Cody and me drawing pictures at the kitchen table. Thinking about it, I can almost smell the strong coffee brewing and the rich cinnamon of those pastries.

"Do you want to share a cab downtown?" Ava was asking Mom.

"No, thanks," my mother said.

I wondered if she had imagined sharing a cab downtown with Dad while she was in the bathroom on the train, foolishly putting on lipstick and perfume. I found myself wondering what Dad would do if he saw her right now, smelling good and looking almost hopeful. Deep down I knew he would do absolutely nothing. He was married to Ava now. I kissed Mom as fast as I could, gulping a big dose of Chanel Number 5. It was weird standing between Mom and Ava. I just wanted to get out of there.

Cody clung to her leg whispering, "Mama, Mama, don't leave me like this."

I disentangled him. I wanted to get away from my mother and melt into life with my father and Ava. We only had the weekend. Every minute counted.

"Good-bye!" I shouted to her, dragging Cody along by the elbow. Even his sniffling couldn't ruin my mood. I felt lighthearted and happy.

I linked arms with Ava. Everyone who saw us would think she was my mother. "Tell me everything you and Daddy have done since I was here last." I hoped my mother saw me walking out like this, arm in arm with Ava Pomme, the Tart Lady.

Chapter Four

DEAD MOTHERS

arie Taglioni, the famous Italian ballerina, was so famous that they named stuff after her. In Russia, for example, there were Taglioni caramels and cakes and even hairdos. After her last performance in 1842, someone bought her ballet shoes for 200 rubles, cooked them, and served them with a special sauce. Then her fans ate them! That sounds like something people would do for a saint, doesn't it?

Marie Taglioni was also very plain-looking. Her teacher in France said, "Will that little hunchback ever learn how to dance?" And then Marie Taglioni became *the* perfect image of a ballerina. Standing en pointe in her white tutu with her hair parted in the middle and pulled back, wearing a floral wreath. So certainly, I, Madeline Vandermeer, could take it when my gum-chewing second-rate ballet teacher Misty Glenn yelled at me during class: "Madeline, what are you, a chicken? You're holding your arms like you have chicken wings!" If that wasn't bad enough, then Misty Glenn said, "Cluck! Cluck!" and a bunch of girls laughed.

Not Demi Demilakis, a girl in my class. She looked at me with pity. She has these really bulgy eyes, like a frog. Like any minute they might pop right out of her head. She'd just moved here from Cleveland, of all places. I asked her once after class if she knew my old friend Rose Malone and those eyes of her went all bulgy and she said, "She was in my grade at Gilmore!" Demi missed Cleveland. Her father used to take her surfing on polluted Lake Erie and she had her birthday party at the Rock and Roll Hall of Fame. Now she's just a new kid, like me.

Still, I didn't want her pity. When she looked at me that way, I glared at her hard. She shrugged and went back to her lazy arabesques. The girl in front of me was wearing a tie-dyed leotard. Madame would have made her leave class. And the girl in front of her was barefoot. Leave it to my mother to find this place.

"Nice extension!" Misty Glenn said.

It took me a minute to realize she was talking to me. She yelled everything, like a gym teacher.

I knew I had a nice extension. I didn't need Misty Glenn to tell me that. One thing was certain, I was suffering. Sainthood had to be right around the corner.

The next day at school, Mai Mai Fan almost knocked me down in the hallway. She was carrying her cello case and heading for the front door.

"Sorry, Madeline," she called over her shoulder. "I can see you are miserable, but I don't want to miss my bus."

"What bus?" I asked her. She didn't stop, of course. Mai Mai never stopped.

I hurried to catch up with her. "What bus?" I said again.

"My bus to Boston. I have my advanced cello lesson there every Monday afternoon. At the Conservatory," she added. "No one here can teach me anything anymore."

If some kids said these very words, they would be bragging. But not Mai Mai. Her life was a giant list of accomplishments. That's really all she had to talk about. She was excellent at everything.

"Do you take that bus alone?" I asked her.

"Of course. I get off at South Station and get on the Red Line," she said.

She told me every step she took, but I stopped listening. If Mai Mai Fan, age eleven — she had skipped a grade — could take a bus and a subway to Boston and back by herself, then surely so could I.

"Now you look happy," Mai Mai said. "Good."

She ran out the door, and disappeared.

"No way," my mother said. "No way."

"Mai Mai Fan —" I started, but my mother looked at me all puzzled.

"What?" she said.

"Mai Mai Fan is a who, not a what," I told her. When your daughter has only a couple of friends, you would think a mother might remember their names.

"The chess champion?" my mother said.

"She is only eleven and she takes the bus by herself every Monday."

We were on our way home from school. I hadn't wasted any time. Returning to Madame's class was too important.

"I am the king of the air," Cody said from the backseat. He had on a stupid paper crown that all the kindergarten kids had made that day.

"Then you are the king of exactly nothing," I told him. "Air is nothing."

My mother had already moved on in topics of conversation. "I have to stop at Whole Foods and see if they carry pomegranate molasses. Jessica says everything is pomegranate this year."

"If air is nothing, then why do we say good night to it in *Goodnight Moon*?" Cody said. I could tell he was close to breaking down, and that made me feel slightly better.

With this renewed strength of purpose I said, "Maybe I'll just go and live with Daddy and go to the American Ballet Theatre school." For some peculiar reason, when I said this I felt queasy, not elated.

"She wants me to do an entire pomegranate menu," my mother said with disgust. "As if kids like pomegranates."

I looked at her. I had just threatened to leave home and all she could talk about were pomegranates?

Cody was starting a full-fledged meltdown. "Are those

the little orange things where we have to eat the skin?" he was saying, all panicked.

"No," I said, my voice as sweet as pomegranate molasses, "they're the red things where you eat just the seeds."

"Why do you act this way?" my mother said.

"They *are* the ones where you eat the seeds," I told her. Then I looked out the window. We were driving down Waterman Street and it was clogged with students from Brown University.

"And by the way," I said, "were you even listening to me? I said if you didn't let me go to Boston on the bus by myself then I would go and live with Daddy." That queasy feeling came right back, as soon as I said those words.

My mother stopped the car, right there in the middle of Waterman Street. "Isn't life strange?" she said.

The car behind us honked its horn, but she just sat there, shaking her head.

"You know I don't like seeds," Cody was crying. "Or skin on fruit. Or fuzzy fruit like kiwi and peaches."

The car behind us squeezed past, and the driver swore at my mother.

"Have you ever heard of Persephone?" my mother asked me.

"Uh, no," I said. I was starting to feel a little nervous. Also, I didn't like not knowing something.

"Persephone was a Greek goddess and she got kidnapped by the god of the underworld. Her mother, whose name I can't remember, was devastated, and eventually Zeus sent someone to rescue Persephone. But she ate these three pomegranate seeds and that forced her to return to the underworld every year for one month for each seed she ate. Three seeds. Three months. That's winter."

More cars were honking now.

My mother looked at me, satisfied. "That is an allegory for what is going on in this car, Madeline," she said, and she started to drive again.

I wanted to ask her what an allegory was. In Humanities we had just covered onomatopoeia and similes, not allegories. But I knew what she'd say. *Look it up.*

Ever since my father married Ava and went on to have a real life, I have had to do a lot of thinking. In science, Mr. Renault calls that developing the power of observation:

watching something and drawing conclusions from what you see. Like we watched snails for weeks in science class. You would be amazed what you can learn from watching a bunch of snails. I had the misfortune of being paired up with Michael Montana, who smells like a wet sweater even when he's not wearing a sweater. His powers of observation, however, are incredible. He can tell snail poop from gravel in a nanosecond. I let him take the notes so that I could better my own powers of observation.

"Once you have developed your powers of observation here in the laboratory," Mr. Renault told us, "you can use them anywhere in the outside world." He seemed to be talking to me when he said, "Use them in your own habitat, for example." The most important thing I observed about my own habitat was that my mother was not living a real life. She was all alone and wrote stuff that people read in doctors' offices months late and only then out of boredom. She wrote things she didn't even believe in herself. In essence, she lied.

Take that stupid article about strawberries and Easy-Make Jelly, Strawberry Shortcake, and a snack of Strawberries Dipped in Yogurt and Brown Sugar. It was true that she dragged us to a strawberry patch one blistering hot summer afternoon. Bees and mosquitoes buzzed all around us, annoying me and scaring Cody. We picked and picked, a boring few hours spent awkwardly bent over, getting dirt in our fingernails. Then we had to go home and eat so many strawberries and strawberry pies, cakes, waffles, and preserves that Cody broke out in hives and had to take oatmeal baths for a week.

But did the article mention any of that? Of course not. It talked about the joys of being outdoors picking stupid strawberries. It never mentioned the bees or the hot sun or any of the true things. In it, a phony family sits in a field somewhere surrounded by strawberries, every one of them grinning like a bunch of idiots. My mother works so hard at making up a life, she never spends time on the one she really has. I used to think her articles were kind of cute. Corny, but cute. That was when we were a happy family. Now I feel like we're no different than the phony family in the pictures.

However, my powers of observation revealed that my father's life really was like something out of a magazine. He had a beautiful wife who smelled like something exotic and romantic and took me to shops in the East Village to try on platform shoes and black miniskirts. He had a real career where he could write about true things that mattered to the world.

When I told my father that I was going to come and live with him if Mom didn't let me take the bus to Boston like Mai Mai Fan, he said, "Madeline, I will convince your mother to let you take that bus. Don't worry."

"But if she says no, absolutely not, I can come and live with you, right?" I said.

"This may not be the most opportune time for that," he said.

My stomach got that queasy feeling again. "You mean I can't live with you?" I said.

"This is a moot point, because you will be on that bus and back at Madame's in no time."

"A what?" I said, wondering how I would ever learn all of these vocabulary words.

"Look it up," he said.

I know that ballerinas and saints have to sacrifice a lot and suffer both physically and mentally. Maybe I would become the Patron Saint of Ballerinas and ballerinas from all over the world would leave me offerings of toe shoes and leg warmers.

I decided to write another letter to the Pope. I told him about my idea. I told him I would be in Italy in June. I signed the letter, *The Future Patron Saint of Ballerinas*. Then, because that sounded a little too smug, I added a question mark. Then an exclamation point. Then I mailed it and waited for him to answer.

When we lived in Boston, I had three best friends — the girls with flower names — and eight regular friends, which made eleven friends total. Eleven friends was the perfect amount. But when we moved to Providence I had exactly no best friends. Sometimes I got invited to someone's house after school, but it never worked out. I would tell them about my miracles and they would want to watch reruns of *Friends*. I would discuss various saints; they would discuss *Teen Vogue*.

For a while I thought Eliza Harrison would be my best friend. Her mother is my mother's best friend — read: only friend — here. While our mothers sit in the Harrisons' basement drinking white wine, Eliza and I go up to her room on the third floor. She has the whole floor, which sounds very fancy, but it's really the attic of their house, so it's just a big open space covered with stuff from Target. She pronounces it *Tar-jay*, which is really annoying. Eliza should go and work at Target because she loves it so much.

One day she said, "Have you seen the dollar bins at Tar-jay? I got all this stuff for pedicures there and it only cost thirteen dollars."

When I didn't answer because I didn't really know what to say to that ridiculous piece of information, Eliza said, "Duh, all of these things were only a dollar each."

I said, "I hate Target." This wasn't actually true. I am neutral about Target.

"Madeline," Eliza said, "why do you have to be so weird?"

This was from a girl who wore peds with her sneakers, those strange little socks they make you use in shoe stores to try on shoes. Eliza also only read books on the summer reading list; she had no imagination. Also, she played field hockey all the time. In the summer she went away to field hockey camp and during the school year she played field hockey on about a thousand different teams. Her thighs looked like tree trunks. I could have told her that. I could have pointed out my own delicate legs, how ballet gave you grace and poise while field hockey only allowed you to run around with a stick and get thick thighs. But I didn't. Instead, I acted saintly.

I said, "Eliza, when I am a saint we'll see who's weird," which made no sense but it was the only thing I could say without crying from frustration.

When my mother finally finished drinking wine with Mrs. Harrison and we went home, instead of giving me sympathy, she said, "Maybe she's giving you a helpful hint."

"Not everything fits under a magazine headline," I told her. "You can't buy a personality at Tar-jay." Then I said, "I bet Daddy would understand."

"Your father," my mother said, shaking her head, "has ruined everything for everybody."

I started to go to church every Sunday. My mother thought I was just getting some fresh air, something she put far too much value in. My research revealed that even though I hated to admit it, she had been right about something: Saints were all Catholic. So Catholic that they died defending the religion. These were called martyrs. I liked the idea of martyrdom, but I didn't want to die. So I started giving up little things: Twizzlers, for one. Sleeping late on Sundays, for another. Instead of staying in my bed, piled up with blankets the way I liked, I got up and put on a nice skirt, and went to church.

One day in spring, with everything draped in purple for Lent and somber white lilies up on the altar, I found myself sitting next to Antoinetta Calabro. The first thing I noticed about her was that she was alone, too, like me. Most kids our age were squeezed into pews with their parents and little sisters and brothers. The next thing I noticed was how different she looked from anyone else I knew.

Antoinetta had long dark hair that fell in about a million curls all around her head. Her nose had a bump on the bridge, smack in the middle, and her eyebrows were dark and heavy. She was the most beautiful girl I had ever seen. Much more beautiful than the pale blond Sophie from next door, or Eliza Harrison with her short bob and perky smile. Antoinetta had an air of tragedy around her, like she had already suffered a great deal. Like she was a martyr.

During the Lamb of God part, Antoinetta finally noticed me looking at her and she frowned. Another good thing:

She took church seriously. I watched her solemnly walk up to get her communion. If only I were Catholic, I could go up there, too, walking as slow and steady as this girl, head bowed, my mind preparing to receive the body of Christ.

When the mass ended, Antoinetta slid out of the pew so quickly that I had to run to catch her.

"Hey!" I said at the front. "I'm Madeline. Do you want to go get a hot chocolate or something?"

"I'm Antoinetta Calabro," she said, shaking her head. "My father's out in the car waiting. He doesn't come in anymore."

"He just sits in the car?"

"Ever since my mother died he says he doesn't believe in church anymore. After he went to San Giovanni Rotundo and made an offering for her to get better and she died, anyway, he says he doesn't believe in anything anymore." She sighed. "He will, though. He just needs time. That's what faith is, right?"

She started to walk out again but I grabbed the sleeve of her beautifully ugly purple coat and stopped her.

"Please," I said. "Maybe I could come home with you or something. I need to talk to you."

"To me?" She looked completely surprised, as if no one ever needed to talk to her. I wasn't letting go, so she shrugged. "Okay," she said.

Out in front in a big Oldsmobile, Antoinetta's father was waiting. He had a droopy, sad face, a dead wife, a car that smelled of stale smoke, and a Christmas-tree air freshener. I thought this must be exactly what heaven was like.

I closed the back door firmly and settled in the backseat alone, so happy I practically started humming the Ave Maria, my all-time favorite hymn. Also the only one I knew. When I glanced up, he was staring at me in the rearview mirror, puzzled.

"I'm Madeline Vandermeer," I said. "Pleased to meet you."

"What are you? Dutch?" he said. His voice was gruff and gravelly.

"A little," I said. That was one of the oddest questions I'd ever been asked. "Also Scotch, Irish, and German."

He laughed. "A Heinz 57!"

What a weirdo, I thought. Then I remembered the dead wife and forgave him.

Neither Antoinetta nor her father wore seat belts. I considered unbuckling mine, too, but I couldn't bring myself to do it. These people were definitely martyrs, I thought. I was practically giddy. From where I sat I had a perfect view of the father's head. He was mostly bald on top, with just a few strands of black hair. Still, it looked like he had put on some kind of hair cream to keep that little bit in place, and to make it shiny. He reminded me of Sonny Bono, the same hangdog face. Sonny Bono and his wife, Cher, were famous in the 60s, a husband-and-wife singing team who ended up also getting divorced. Then Sonny Bono skied into a tree and died, but by then Cher had married a bunch of other people and Sonny had a wife and a new kid. My parents had all of Sonny and Cher's albums. On car trips, they used to sing "I Got You, Babe," my mother singing Cher's parts and my father singing Sonny's. My mother got the albums in the divorce, but she doesn't play them anymore.

"Wasn't that sad when Sonny Bono died?" I said, because he reminded me of him and also because no one else was saying anything.

"You go to school with Antoinetta?"

"Uh," I said. "No."

"I know her from church," Antoinetta said.

I watched as we passed the State House, which everyone always got so excited about.

"Third largest unsupported dome in the world," I said, showing off.

"What's that supposed to mean?" Mr. Calabro said suspiciously.

"You know, the roof," I said. "The dome."

He squinted at me in the rearview mirror and I squirmed. I decided not to tell him the other two, which were the Capitol Building in Washington, D.C., and, my favorite, Saint Peter's Cathedral in Rome.

We were going past the Castle Cinema, the second-run movie theater on Chalkstone Boulevard. I didn't know anyone who lived in this part of Providence. It was almost like being in another country. We stopped in front of a three-story blue house. Right there, on the front lawn, a statue of the Virgin Mary was standing in what appeared to be an open oyster shell. A shrine! I was elated.

"I love your house," I said, and meant it.

Antoinetta's father looked at me like I was crazy again. Then he went inside.

"So," Antoinetta said. Then she just stood there in that purple coat. It had big black buttons and every one looked like it was about to fall off.

Even though it was almost Easter, there were still some patches of snow in the front yard and when I talked, puffs of air came out. There was a candle lit in the shrine and some artificial flowers in an empty Fresca bottle.

"What happened to your mother?" I asked her.

"Female trouble," Antoinetta said.

That sounded really saintly. "Did she have hospice?"

"Nah. The doctor wanted her to but my father kept saying she was going to get better. Because of the miracle, you know? San Giovanni Rotundo."

I could only nod. Something much larger than me, something divine, had led me to this girl, this house.

"Want to go inside?"

"Yes," I said so eagerly that Antonietta shook her head.

We walked up three steps into the house, entering a hallway that had lots of boots and coats and umbrellas, two closed doors, and a stairway leading to the second floor.

"We live up there, but it's Sunday so we go to my grandmother's," Antonietta said. She put her hand on the doorknob, then turned to me. "Are you staying for lunch?"

"Great!" I said. "Thanks." I couldn't believe my good fortune. I thought of all the other things I might have been doing today — being forced to read the funnies to Cody or going to the mall with Eliza Harrison, watching her try on clothes at the Gap. But I was here instead. I made a very quick sign of the cross, a thank-you of sorts. I always did them fast because I wasn't sure I knew the right way.

Antoinetta opened the door onto the most beautiful room I had ever seen. I had seen all kinds of houses that everyone thought were beautiful: the restored Victorians like Sophie's with their stained glass windows and polished hardwood floors; the modern ones like Eliza Harrison's with wall-to-wall carpeting and an all-white kitchen; the large Colonials like Nana Vandermeer lived in, all polished silver and heavy antique furniture. But never had I seen anything like this. My powers of observation told me I would never see anything like it again.

We were in the living room and all of the furniture was covered with plastic. Under the plastic, the sofa was maroon; on top of the plastic were round pillows in crocheted covers of gold and white, purple and red, an array of dizzying colors. There were lamps with goddesses dancing around their base and plastic covering the lampshades. Every table had ashtrays, big elaborate orange ones filled with ashes and cigarette butts. The drapes were gold and heavy. In the corner was another saint. I knew it was Saint Francis of Assisi because he was surrounded by animals.

Even though this seemed to be the biggest room downstairs, everyone was jammed into the kitchen, where smells like the ones at Francesco's Restaurant in New York floated out. There wasn't one book in sight, I realized, as I followed Antoinetta to the kitchen. Just a *TV Guide* sitting on top of the television beside a line of pictures: a wedding photograph, a man in a World War II uniform, and a close-up of a woman who looked like a movie star from the forties, all black-and-white. The soldier's picture had crystal rosary beads wrapped around it, the silver cross dangling over his right shoulder.

"That's my uncle Curly," she whispered. "He died in the war."

She took me by the elbow and led me into the kitchen. More dazzling sights: an old woman with bobby pins all over her thinning hair, frying sausage at the stove. Small children eating meatballs without any sauce on them, fat babies in rickety high chairs drinking orange juice from sippy cups. Women, all with Antoinetta's luxuriant black hair and full figures, dressed in stockings and high heels and snug dresses, all with gold crosses around their necks, all talking while they cut spinach pie into slabs, pulled pigs in a blanket from the oven, put slices of homemade pizza on a platter. The men sat around the table, which was covered with heavy yellow plastic, smoking and drinking something clear out of small glasses, not talking, but eating as the food appeared on the table.

"This is my friend Madeline . . ." Antoinetta paused and looked at me. "Van Mars," she said finally, and I didn't even care that she got my name wrong. "We're going to go upstairs until lunch is ready."

No! I wanted to tell her. *I want to stay here!*

"Want to take a piece of pizza?" Antoinetta said, putting two on a pink plastic plate without waiting for an answer. She put some spinach pie on it, too. "Come on."

Antoinetta and her father and sister's apartment upstairs was dark and quiet. It smelled stale, like the windows hadn't been opened in about a hundred years. The quiet up there felt like it had started a long time ago; it made me whisper.

"Want to see a picture of my mother?" Antoinetta said in a normal voice, chewing her pizza.

"Sure," I whispered.

I had never known anyone whose mother was actually dead. At my old school, there was a girl whose mother had died a long time ago but she had a stepmother and didn't seem very tragic. But Antoinetta was different, I could tell. We walked through the living room — more plastic-covered furniture and another saint statue — I didn't recognize this one but I could see it had been broken and glued back together. There were thin lines all over it, like veins.

In her bedroom, Antoinetta handed me a picture from her bureau. The woman had curly hair like Antoinetta's, and full lips with red lipstick. She was sexy and pretty and full of life. I shivered.

"Wow," I said, still whispering.

Antoinetta took back the picture, but instead of putting it down she studied it, too. "She was sick forever. Practically my whole life she was sick. I don't remember her doing very much. My sister does."

She put the picture down and added, "She's older."

"I'm going to Italy," I said.

"To San Giovanni Rotundo?"

"I don't know. Maybe. My mother's planning the trip." Immediately, I felt bad for saying that. How thoughtless to mention an alive mother to Antoinetta. "She's divorced," I said, hoping that made up for the other remark.

Antoinetta was frowning. "Aren't you Catholic?"

"Sort of. I mean, I am but she's not."

"The Pope doesn't let people get divorced," Antoinetta said, still frowning. "It's a sin."

"She's Unitarian," I said.

"What's that? Protestant?"

"Not exactly," I said. I was afraid if I said the wrong thing Antoinetta wouldn't be my friend. "It's kind of its own thing."

"So who's sick?"

"Huh?"

"You go to San Giovanni Rotundo for a miracle. Don't you know?"

I shook my head.

Antoinetta sighed, frustrated. "Padre Pio was this priest who could heal people. In Italy. Like if your mother or some-body was sick right here he could come to her bedside even though he was saying a mass in Italy at the very same time. He could be in two places at once. If you go there, there's a whole chapel with the crutches and braces and things from people he healed. And letters from people. I don't know why he couldn't heal my mother."

"Did you meet him?"

Antoinetta laughed. "He's dead, silly. You pray for him to intercede on your behalf. You know, ask God for the favor. My grandmother said that God wanted my mother with him. So he refused Padre Pio's request."

I considered this possibility.

Then Antoinetta spoke in a low voice. "They called us up and told us to come to the hospital. It was only four o'clock in the morning and my father took us in our pajamas and we got there in time to hear the priest give her the Sacrament of the Sick and then just sat there waiting for the miracle to happen, you know? That whole time she would only take a breath every minute or so. I was holding my breath until she took her next one. And then, she just didn't take another one. It was 5:03. I looked at the clock. Everybody started screaming and my father cursed the Virgin Mary and Padre

Pio and the doctors. Because we'd gone all that way. For a miracle, you know?"

I nodded, remembering my own miracle, how I saved my father from the avalanche. This wasn't the time to tell Antoinetta. But I would. Antoinetta was the one person who could understand.

"My mother's patron saint was Saint Clare. She was named for her. When we got home from the hospital, my father picked up my mother's statue of Saint Clare, the one the bishop blessed, and he threw it against the wall. My uncle Joe glued it back together."

"Saint Clare," I said. "She's the patron saint of television."

Antoinetta smiled at me. "Want to play saints? You pick one to be and I'll pick one and we'll pretend we're dying?"

My heart soared. "Yes," I said.

Chapter Five

ALL THE MISTAKES

Thanks to my father's divine intervention, I auditioned for the junior company of the Boston Ballet. If I got picked, I would take the bus into Boston twice a week for class, starting in September. My feet hurt from my toe shoes and my neck hurt from stretching so much. In other words, I felt great. Each of us waited in a big room, and they called our names one by one. When it was my turn, I stood all alone up on the stage and official people with notepads out in the audience asked me to do this or that. *Jeté! Arabesque! Jumps in first position! In fifth! Switch! Switch!* I had a good audition. I knew it. When I walked off the stage, one of the women shouted, "Thanks, Madeline! You'll be hearing from us!" in a way that made me think: *I got it!*

But when I went out to the waiting room where all the mothers were sitting, I acted very cool. I saw them trying to read my face, but I wanted to seem mysterious. I mean, would Marie Taglioni rush out after an audition and start bragging and gushing? No. She would have good posture. She would nod. She would leave.

"Well?" my mother whispered as I gathered up my things. When I didn't answer, she said, "Madeline? I'm dying here." That made me smile.

I almost took her hand while we rushed down the long corridor and then the stairs that led us outside. But I didn't want to be seen, a future ballerina with the junior company of the Boston Ballet, holding hands with my mother. So I just made a face that said: *I think I got it!* And in that instant, when her eyes lit up with something like pride, I almost loved her with the same intensity I used to before the divorce.

Once we got outside, though, and the car cost a zillion dollars to park in the garage and the traffic was thick and cars cut us off and honked their horns, I went back to being annoyed with her. I knew better than to distract her, even about this, when she was driving in Boston traffic.

So I put in my new favorite tape. Nuns singing Renaissance music.

"Do we have to listen to this now?" my mother said. She gripped the steering wheel hard enough that her knuckles got white and bony. "Can't we listen to whoever kids are really listening to these days?"

"I like nuns," I said. I wanted her to get us out of the traffic and concentrate on my audition even more, so I just listened to the nuns and thought about when we all lived in Boston and were happy. I thought about my Montessori School and how there were no grades and kids were put together by what they knew and what they liked. I was in the Ocean group. We read stories about the sea and kept a tank of saltwater tropical fish and learned about underwater life. Where were they now, the Ocean group? I wondered. I tried to remember their faces, the kid with the freckles, the kid from Germany, the boy who said he wanted to marry me. And my three friends with the beautiful flower names.

I sighed, homesick for our old life, the way we would cook spaghetti together and my father would make one of his super-duper salads and play opera and we would all sing together real loud. Sometimes I had dreams where I was in that apartment and someone was singing *"L'amour est un oiseau rebelle"* from *Carmen* but it wasn't my mother singing and it wasn't my father; in fact, I couldn't find either of them and I couldn't find my way, either. I hated that dream.

"At last," my mother said, relaxing. "Okay. Tell me about it. Every detail."

But I wasn't thinking about the audition anymore. Instead, I was thinking about the Calabros and how they'd invited me over for Easter breakfast. *Bring your mother,* they'd said.

"Want to go somewhere with me?" I said, surprising myself because the last thing I wanted was to share the Calabros with my mother. But thinking about our old life had made me forget for a minute how much I didn't like her anymore.

"It depends," she said.

"Can't you just say yes? I mean it's a thing I want you to do and right away you have to have all these conditions."

"All right. I'll do it. But can't I even ask what it is?"

I was already sorry I'd invited her. I tried to think of a lie, to make up something like the school carnival or something. But that might be a sin. It was so hard to be Catholic.

"This is a mistake," I said. Our life seemed to be gathering mistakes at a surprising speed.

"Come on," my mother said.

"I have this new friend," I said reluctantly. I saw it already, a new mistake coming. "Antoinetta."

"Antoinetta?"

"Antoinetta," I said, clenching my teeth. "And her family invited us for Easter breakfast."

"All of us?"

I frowned. "Not your boyfriend. Us. Our family."

"I was thinking of Cody," my mother said gently.

I thought of all the kids that roamed around the Calabro house every Sunday, the little ones eating meatballs and the fat babies and then the middle ones, girls who chewed gum and braided one another's hair and put on temporary tattoos.

"Cody can come," I said.

"Should I call her mother and ask her what I can bring?"

"Her mother's dead," I said proudly.

"Well, isn't that sad," she said.

"Yeah," I said, but thinking about the Calabros, I didn't feel sad at all. Instead, I felt part of something I hadn't felt part of for a long time: a family.

Right away I saw it had been a mistake to bring my mother. For one thing, she wore a suit, the kind of thing she wore to meetings with editors. For another, she had brought asparagus with toasted sesame oil. I looked at her standing there in her business clothes, holding the pottery dish with the scrawny asparagus in it, and I wanted to disappear. Better yet, I wanted her to disappear.

But Mama Angie, Antoinetta's grandmother, came over and took the dish. She smelled it, then said to my mother, "You're Dutch, right?"

"No. No. I'm just American, I guess."

"Indians?"

"I'm nothing," my mother said, laughing.

"Huh," Mama Angie said, and she put the asparagus in the refrigerator.

I brought my mother and Cody into the kitchen and introduced them to all the aunts and uncles, and to Antoinetta's father, and to Antoinetta herself. She was wearing a yellow ruffly dress. Antoinetta dressed pretty badly, but I didn't care. She went to Catholic school and wore a blue plaid jumper or a skirt with a white blouse, a navy cardigan, and either navy kneesocks or tights every day. She didn't have to think about clothes. She could use her brain cells to think about religion, about saints and things.

Cody was with the little kids. Mama Angie had made him a little loaf of sweetbread, like she did for her own grandchildren, in the shape of a cross. Smack in the middle was a boiled egg. One of the aunts — Carla? Fanny? I still couldn't keep them straight — was showing my mother the special Easter breakfast foods: the homemade cheese and the frittata, which was like an omelette, and the pastera, which was a rice pie.

"This is so interesting," my mother was saying. "Did you know I have a cooking column? And my project now is ethnic food."

"Yeah? Who do you write that for? *Good Housekeeping?*"

"No —"

"*Ladies' Home Journal?*"

"No. It's a magazine called *Family.*"

"I never heard of it," the aunt said, and went back to layering a lasagna.

Mostly, during breakfast, I was miserable. My mother kept embarrassing me. It was like she was incapable of doing or saying anything right these days. Who cared about her stupid column? Worst of all, she didn't even realize how she was coming across.

Now she was asking Aunt Mary how they made the pastera. "We don't tell strangers our recipes," Aunt Mary said coldly. I couldn't believe what was happening.

Then she went over to Antoinetta's father and asked him stupid questions about being a barber, and when he answered them she gushed, "How interesting!"

She even tried to explain Unitarianism to two of the uncles.

"You got the Father, the Son, and the Holy Ghost. You understanding what I am saying?" Uncle Al said.

"Well, yes," my mother said. "But —"

"There is no but," he said. "That's what you got."

Then, Mama Angie, all four foot ten of her, climbed onto the kitchen table. She took a bottle of holy water from her apron pocket and sprayed it over all our heads, saying something in Italian.

Still on the table, she called to me, "You staying for lunch? We got lasagna."

I felt so proud, being singled out like that by Mama Angie, but my mother had to open her big mouth. "We couldn't possibly eat one more thing. But thank you."

Antoinetta pulled me into the hallway while my mother went around shaking everyone's hand like she had just gotten a new magazine assignment.

"I had the most incredible idea," Antoinetta said. "Wouldn't it be great if my father fell in love with your mother?"

I almost laughed. "You've got to be kidding," I said.

"What's wrong with my father?"

"Nothing," I said. "It's just that what would he ever see in my mother?"

Antoinetta looked at me, shocked. "But she's so beautiful," she said.

I watched my mother coming toward us, holding Cody's hand in one hand and the dish with the asparagus in the other. No one had even tried it.

"She is?" I said, seeing nothing but a person who messed up everything she touched.

In the car on the way home Mom said, "How do you know this girl?"

"Church," I said.

"What church?"

I shrugged.

Then Cody, who had eaten his entire miniature loaf of bread, pizza, two slices of pastera, canned pineapple, and ham, said he was carsick.

"It was a mistake to let you eat so much strange food," my mother, the expert on ethnic cuisine, said, swerving into the breakdown lane.

She took Cody out of the car and stood way over near the scrub that grew by the road. I watched them, Cody's face with its greenish cast, my mother in her silly business suit.

She saw me looking and waved like an idiot.

"We're okay!" she shouted.

"No, we're not," I said to myself.

Chapter Six

BETRAYALS

Even though my house and my mother and my little brother were the biggest embarrassments in my life, I invited Antoinetta to sleep over on a Saturday night. I had to.

For one thing, my mother didn't like that I was always at Antoinetta's house. "Don't girls take turns hosting each other?" she said, which made her sound like Martha Stewart. For another thing, even though I went to her house every Sunday after church, her father didn't allow sleepovers there. "Strangers in our house at night make him uncomfortable," Antoinetta explained, which insulted me. After all, I wasn't exactly a stranger. When I said that to Antoinetta she got all defensive. "He's suspicious of things like that," she said.

"That's all." So if I was going to get Antoinetta to myself for a whole night it had to be in my awful house with my awful family. That definitely went on my merit list for sainthood.

It took weeks to convince her father that this was a good idea. He asked her questions like: "What will you eat over there?" and "What do these people want from you?" After the asparagus incident I could understand the food question. But I was beginning to think that maybe Antoinetta's father was *paranoid*, which meant he believed everybody was after him — that was a bonus vocabulary word and I got it right.

By the time he gave her permission, I was deep into rehearsals for that ballet set to Vivaldi's *Four Seasons.* This was for Misty Glenn. And I got the lead in "Spring," even with my so-called chicken arms. It required great concentration and practice. Also, I had just started dancing in toe shoes and my feet killed me. When I took off my toe shoes my big toes were all bloody. I liked to come home and soak my feet. I even let my mother wrap my toes in soft gauze, which made me feel good. She was so gentle and nice when she did it, and all the while I thought of the pain I was enduring and how good that was for my pending sainthood, too.

So even though it was the most inconvenient time in the world for me to have someone sleep over, since that someone was Antoinetta, I got all excited. At rehearsal, the choreographer, a man named Randy, told me I was not concentrating hard enough. I missed my cue twice and I did a sloppy arabesque. My jumps, he said, gave him indigestion. Randy spoke with a mysterious accent, and Demi Demilakis, who got the lead in "Winter," said that she'd heard he was from Transylvania. This sounded both scary and exciting to me.

Before I could leave, Randy stopped me at the door. "It is Spring," he said, frowning. "You must think light! Think airy! You must think!"

I stood there, clutching my ballet bag, my toes aching like crazy. I concentrated on my costume, all sparkling green and glittery in its plastic wrap, in my other hand. I wished I could explain everything to him. I wondered where Transylvania was, and decided it must be in Russia. Then I wondered if there were any Russian saints. The only thing I knew about Russia was from seeing half of *Doctor Zhivago*, which was probably the most boring movie ever made. My mother cried through the whole thing and made terrible soup called borscht for dinner afterward. Borscht is beets, which are the worst vegetables, worse even than cauliflower.

"Madeline?" Randy said. He rapped my head with his knuckles, hard. "What is going on in there?"

I shrugged, thinking that maybe all Russians were saints — all the snow, all those beets. They endured an awful lot. I wondered if I had a crush on Randy, with his sunken eyes and Gumby body and his weird accent.

"Is Transylvania in Russia?" I asked him.

"I have no idea," he said, clearly disgusted with me.

When my mother and I got home, Antoinetta and her father were already there, an hour early, sitting in their car.

"Is that them?" my mother said, sounding distressed. "Already?"

Limping, I followed her to their car.

"Hello," she said in her fakest voice. "Would you like to come in?"

"Yes," Antoinetta said too quickly. "He would."

I practically groaned out loud. Antoinetta still thought her father and my mother might get together, even after I explained I could never do that to her or her father.

Luckily, he refused to come in. He didn't like to go into other people's houses. He actually said that to my mother.

Even with my sore feet and bad rehearsal, having Antoinetta for a whole night made me the happiest I had felt in a long time. My mother was asking us questions about beverages and dinner and renting movies, but we didn't stop to answer. Instead, I grabbed on to Antoinetta's arm and pulled her upstairs.

Antoinetta brought her book, *The Lives of the Saints*, and we took turns reading about different ones and acting out the best parts of their lives: getting our eyes plucked out, burning to death, helping lepers. Being a saint was exhausting.

"You know," Antoinetta whispered after we got in bed and turned off the lights, "I might become a nun."

I frowned. "You can't get married or anything," I said.

"You marry Jesus," she said, shocked at my stupidity. "You wear a wedding dress and everything."

"But you don't get to kiss anybody," I said.

"You get to be Jesus's bride," she said. Her voice had turned cold. "That's better than kissing anything."

"Okay," I said, suddenly bored and sleepy.

"Boys smell bad. Like dirty socks," she said. "Jesus is clean and pure."

When I didn't answer her she rolled away from me. But what could I say? I wanted to skip the nun part and go straight to saint; that was a fact. Along the way I might want to kiss a boy, a real boy, smelly or not.

"You'd be a good nun," I said finally.

She didn't answer but somehow I knew she wasn't asleep.

"Really," I said. "You would be a great nun."

She rolled over again, toward me so that we were face-to-face. When she talked, I could smell the pepperoni from the pizza we'd had for dinner on her breath.

"I might be an airline stewardess instead," she whispered. "Then I would marry a pilot and live in Chicago."

I mumbled something. My toes ached in a way that I liked.

"You know Joseph Copertino?" Antoinetta said. Clearly, she had not been dancing ballet all day or she would just be quiet and go to sleep.

"Is he from church?" I asked her.

Antoinetta laughed. "No, silly. He's the patron saint of air travel. Ever since he was a kid, he had these ecstasies. Yelling, beating, pinching, burning, piercing with needles — none of this would bring him out of them. But he would return to the world when he heard the voice of his boss." She yawned. "He would often levitate and float, so he became the patron saint of air travel." She rolled over. "Mmmmm," she said. "Hmhmhmhm."

I guessed those were falling asleep noises. But now I was wide awake. Floating! Levitating! I lay there, concentrating really hard on getting my body to lift up from the bed. But I just stayed there, earthbound, until I finally gave up and went to sleep.

The next day, Cody was going to Henrietta Plotz's birthday pool party at her house. She had a pizza shaped like a dinosaur and a karaoke machine. That was all fine for Cody, but why I had to go was beyond me. I didn't even care that they had an indoor pool.

"Bianca got to ask one person her age and she picked you," my mother explained, talking like this was a good thing for me.

Henrietta's sister Bianca was so dull and so unliked that the fact that she had picked me made me certain that the *L* on my forehead was getting bigger every day.

"Besides," my mother said, "saints are into sacrifice, aren't they? You should feel grateful for the opportunity to give up an afternoon this way."

"Ha-ha," I said. But she had a point.

That's how I ended up at a six-year-old's party, sitting on the side of the pool with Bianca Plotz looking at the younger kids splashing around. I could see my mother, sitting with the other mothers, in her pants with the drawstring waist and her toenails painted baby blue and only the top of her black bathing suit. She was telling them how my father did not want her to take us away so far for so long.

"He's being a jerk," she said.

Cody floated on his back. It was all he could do. Everyone else graduated in swimming class, from Pike to Eel to Minnow, and Cody remained behind, unable to put his face in the water, to blow bubbles, or to kick his feet and move his arms together in a way that would move him forward. He stayed in Pike. He floated.

Cody always wanted to get me on his side about the divorce, which meant that he wanted me to blame Dad for everything. Just that morning he said, "Would you feel really horrible if Ava Pomme died?" Cody always said Ava Pomme like they were two parts of one word: powder puff, coffee cake, Ava Pomme.

"Of course I'd feel bad!" I said. "And so would you."

"But if she died," he said, "then Dad would come home."

As dumb as that was, even I considered the possibility.

"I don't like her," Cody whispered, all sad and guilty.

He made a list of all the things he didn't like about her and decided to recite it to me right then, for about the millionth time. This was a trick he'd picked up from our mother, who had picked it up from her therapist.

"Her tarts," he told me.

"Her tarts," I reminded him, "are famous."

"I only like Pop-Tarts," Cody said. Then he imitated Ava Pomme's horrified voice: "Surely your mother doesn't give you those?"

"Pop-Tarts," I said, jumping to Ava's defense, "are totally revolting."

"Her clothes," Cody continued. "They're black. All of them."

I sighed. "Of course they're black. That's sophisticated." Our mother's wardrobe of various types of khaki trousers — capri, flat front, side zipper, loose fit — floated through my mind.

"The noisy elevator that goes to her apartment," he said.

"Cody," I reminded him, "it goes to *their* apartment."

"It's for deliveries," he practically shouted. "I hate that sliding grate that you have to close after you already closed the door. Then it goes up so slow, and it makes that noise that sounds like at any minute it will break and everyone in it — you and me and stupid Ava Pomme — will smash to death."

Twice Cody had hyperventilated in that elevator, forcing Ava Pomme to stick his head in a bag of tomatoes one time and a bag of sourdough bread the other time. When he caught his breath, he threw up: once in the elevator and once on Ava's black shoes.

"That baby," Cody said. "Zoe."

I frowned.

"Kiss your baby sister," Cody said in his Ava Pomme voice.

Zoe didn't seem real to me. She didn't do much of anything except get carried around and look cute. When I was a baby, my father used to carry me on his back in a big forest green backpack. I had pictures of that, with my parents standing together on a beach somewhere and my own baby face grinning out over my father's shoulder. I loved those pictures. No Cody. No Ava Pomme. No Zoe. Just a family.

The idea that Zoe would one day turn into a person, someone to contend with, made me nervous. I didn't like to think about it.

I hated divorce. It should be illegal or something. All it did was cause problems for everybody. Sometimes I felt like I was getting pecked apart by crows, pieces of me scattered from here to New York. I wished I was still whole, the way I had been before my mother messed up everything.

One time, right after Baby Zoe was born and I was feeling about as low as I ever had, my mother came in my bedroom and found me crying. When she walked in, I put a pillow over my face so she couldn't see me all red and blotchy and sad. She sat on the bed, took the pillow away, and put her cool hand on my forehead, the way she used to when I was little and felt sick to my stomach. "I know, I know," she kept saying, but she didn't know. She didn't know that I thought everything was her fault. She didn't know how it felt to have your father leave and marry some other woman and then have a new baby.

So I told her. I sat up and let the pillow drop to the floor and shook her hand off my forehead and said, "It didn't have to be like this! Why do you go and mess everything up?" She looked shocked. "How did *I* mess everything up?" Mom asked me. "By being so ordinary," I told her. Then she started to cry, too. She said, "Oh, Madeline." In a movie, we would have cried together, in each other's arms. But this was real life. Mom got up slowly and shook her head and walked out of the room, and I was left alone to think about everything, which now included not just divorced parents and a stepmother, but also a baby sister.

Here she was now, casting a shadow over me.

"Time to go," Mom said, still in her bathing suit.

"Fine," I said. Three hours at this stupid kid party and boring Bianca had hardly said a word. She was traumatized because she was going to sleepover camp next week and she had never been away from her parents. How lame is that?

She should try never ever getting to spend real days with her father. She should try having everything good being stuck in a photograph instead of part of her real life.

"Bye, Bianca," I said.

"Are you going to write me at camp?" she said desperately.

What would I ever write to her? "Gee," I said.

"Of course she will," my mother said. "She'll send you postcards from Italy."

My mother and I stood for a minute, side by side, watching Cody float.

"I am not going to write her at camp," I said.

"She's lonely," my mother said, her eyes fixed on Cody. "You have no idea what loneliness feels like."

"Here we go again," I mumbled.

"Hey, buddy," my mother called to Cody. "Let's go."

Slowly, he floated to the edge of the pool, near the ladder. She held out the big blue-and-red striped towel that had his name printed in the middle in bright yellow letters. She was smiling, her arms outstretched.

Cody ran into the towel, into her arms.

"I can't wait to go to Italy," he said.

Our mother looked startled. "Good," she said. Then she nodded. "Good," she said again, as if she had just won something.

How could he give in like that? Secretly I had been imagining meeting the Pope, praying to saints, going to all the churches. But I had not let my mother know that, of course.

Cody and I never liked the Friday night dinners our mother made us eat. This Friday was even worse: The Boyfriend was joining us. Cody sat at the kitchen counter, watching her cook, sullen. I sat at the table trying to move a glass of water across it using telepathy. Too much distraction, I thought. Too many bad vibrations.

Our mother said, "Is there anything in the world as lovely as the smell of fresh basil?"

We weren't expected to answer. Our mother had asked what was called a rhetorical question. But Cody said, "Peanut butter."

"Peanut butter smells as good as basil?" she shrieked. "Oh, that's a good one."

I rolled my eyes at Cody. We didn't agree on many things. But we both agreed that Friday night dinners were awful. We also agreed that our mother should not have a boyfriend. Especially this boyfriend. Things were already weird enough in our life.

She put a bowl of celery sticks on the table. I bit into one right away and spit it out. A trick! Instead of celery this tasted like licorice without the good candy part.

"Fennel," my sadistic mother said, smiling. "Isn't it an interesting celery substitute?"

"No," I said, just as sweetly. "It's disgusting and repulsive."

I knew she didn't care. She would write in her column how much we'd loved it and then other unsuspecting mothers would give fennel sticks to their children. She would write something like, "They'll be delighted at the surprise taste of licorice instead of the blandness of celery."

She was humming, not really paying attention to my misery.

"What time is The Boyfriend getting here?" I muttered.

My mother narrowed her eyes at me. "Why do you work so hard at being unpleasant?" she said.

What I worked hard at was being *pleasant*, but I didn't say anything. I just stripped the long threads from the stalks of fennel.

"If I were a sculptor," Cody said, "I would make things out of metal so they couldn't break. What good is making things that no one can touch?"

"No one can touch the Sistine Chapel," Mom said. "Does that mean Michelangelo shouldn't have painted it?"

Cody frowned. He didn't know what she was talking about.

The doorbell rang and she tousled Cody's hair on her way to answer it. "You'll see it in Rome," she said.

"It's a ceiling," I told him. "A famous ceiling."

"Uh-huh," Cody said.

Mom turned toward us, her face all desperate, and she said, "You know, your father is soooo happy with his new family and his new life as a celebrity. Am I asking too much to want a little happiness of my own? Am I?"

We just stared at her, surprised and blank-faced. She stared back and I wondered if she was going to cry. But then the doorbell rang again and she scurried off.

We could hear her laughing her new laugh, the one she'd acquired around men lately, full of fakeness and flirtiness.

"Why would anyone waste their time painting a ceiling?" Cody asked me. "How do you even do it?"

I put out bread for a sandwich, inhaling the familiar smell of Wonder Bread. Then I smeared on peanut butter and grape jelly and handed it to Cody.

"Doesn't the paint drip on your face?" Cody was saying.

"He did it on his back," I said patiently.

Cody's eyes widened. "Wasn't he afraid he would fall?"

"No, he was on scaffolding."

Cody looked all confused, but I didn't know how to describe what scaffolding was so I just said, "It's a beautiful, famous ceiling. You'll see."

Then I made my way past my mother and The Boyfriend, heading for the door.

"Hey!" my mother said. "We have polenta."

"Enjoy it," I said. "I'm going next door to Sophie's."

Being at Sophie's was like being in a museum: all fancy and quiet. The rooms were all painted colors that made me feel calm; the floors had intricate patterns made with wood. The kitchen had two of everything — two stoves, two refrigerators, two dishwashers — and cupboards that reached the ceiling. Those cupboards had glass doors so that I could see all of the food Sophie's parents kept on hand. Crackers and chutney and fat pretzels, Little School Boy cookies and Mint Milanos, three different kinds of salsa and smoked almonds. On and on it went. At home there was yogurt and granola bars and bags of dried fruit and trail mix bought in bulk from the natural food store.

Sophie was probably the busiest person on the planet next to Mai Mai Fan. She played field hockey and she took clarinet lessons and horseback riding lessons and a million other lessons. A ballerina has to be focused. A saint has to sacrifice. In other words, I had my hands full, too, just in a different way. Also, my mother believed that kids should not lead overly organized lives.

Sometimes I pointed out that Sophie's mother hired someone to keep her organized and drive her from one thing to another, but of course that only opened the door for my mother's ranting about money and my father and how unfair life is.

"I can't afford an outrageously expensive loft in Tribeca, can I?" she liked to ask me. A rhetorical question.

Sophie's parents were at a play in Boston and wouldn't be home until late. Tonight, Sophie's older sister Emma was in charge, which meant she would sit upstairs on the third floor in her room and read. Emma was an overachiever. She wanted to read one hundred books this summer — an admirable goal, I thought.

"I've got a surprise for you upstairs," Sophie said. "Grab some Snapple."

I opened one of the giant refrigerators. A half-eaten turkey stared back at me.

"Not that one," Sophie laughed. "In the beverage one."

I went to the other refrigerator and swung its heavy door open. Top to bottom drinks: beer and seltzer and fancy root beer and all kinds of milk: skim, 2%, and whole. At my house we only drank skim milk and water from the tap. Finally I found the Snapple and grabbed a bottle.

"Come on," Sophie said, her hands full of snacks for us.

I walked through the double parlors, with the furniture that begged you to sit on it, then into the foyer — *foy-ay*, Sophie called it — and up the big front staircase to the second floor and Sophie's room. Sophie stacked all the food on a table and plopped onto her bed, which looked like a giant sleigh. I plopped next to her, imagining for a moment that we were in Russia, long-ago Russia when they still had a czar and people wore tall fur hats and ermine cloaks, and I imagined we were in a real sleigh, gliding across miles and miles of snow. I sighed. If I didn't already have so many more important things to wish for, I would want to be Russian.

"Ready?" Sophie said.

I glanced over at her. Tonight she had on a lime green headband with one yellow stripe in the middle and small earrings shaped like seashells. My mother would not let me get my ears pierced until I was sixteen. She did not believe girls should think about things like earrings until they got older. I sighed again. I didn't really like Sophie, but being near her always made me long for every single thing I could not have.

"If it's smoking I've already tried it," I said. "In New York with this girl named Lola who already has her belly button pierced and she's only twelve." I tried to sound nonchalant but it was hard. Smoking in New York City on a roof was too cool. Lola was too cool. So cool, in fact, that I was actually afraid of her. She lived in the loft above my father's with just her mother, a performance artist. I wasn't even sure what that meant, but it sounded very dramatic.

"This is better," Sophie said.

Sophie thought everything she did was better but it usually wasn't. She reached under her bed and pulled something out.

"Ta-da!" she said.

I gasped. "A Ouija board." I had to admit it, this *was* better than almost anything.

I swallowed hard, running my hands over the board's slick surface.

"We should turn off the lights," I said.

Sophie went around the room flicking off lights, leaving just the small one beside the bed lit.

"Let's concentrate first," I said. "Try to connect with the spirits."

We both put our hands very lightly on the mover and closed our eyes.

"Concentrate," I said.

I thought about how I'd saved my father's life, how I'd

made that glass slide across the table. Out of the blue, I thought about Antoinetta's dead mother. I wished Antoinetta were here so she could communicate with her mother.

Under our fingertips, the indicator moved ever so slightly.

"Are you doing that?" Sophie whispered.

"No," I said, feeling all trembly. I peeked under my eyelids to see if Sophie was doing it. But she looked pretty worried.

"Should we ask a question?" Sophie said. "Like who we will marry or something?"

I rolled my eyes. I had bigger things on my mind, like miracles. I stared hard at the board. "Is someone with us?" I asked.

The indicator skidded in jerky movements across the board again.

I glanced up at Sophie.

"Are you doing that?" Sophie asked again.

"Why would I move it?" I said. I looked at the board again. "Who are you?" I whispered.

This time the movements were smoother. The small needle went first to *G*, then *R*, *E*, *E*, *R*, where it stopped.

We looked at each other. "Greer," I said, so pleased I could hardly stand it. "It's Mr. Greer."

Sophie's hands flew off the mover. "I don't like this," she said. "I thought it would be like the Magic 8-Ball. That we'd ask who we were going to marry and how many kids we'd have. Stuff like that."

"Come on," I said. "This is better."

Sophie hesitated.

"One more minute," I said.

Reluctantly, Sophie put her fingers back onto the mover.

But before we even asked a question it started to move, so fast that Sophie had to shout out the letters. When it finally stopped, she scribbled them onto a pad for us to interpret.

BEWAREM.

"'Be warm'?" Sophie asked, confused.

But I couldn't speak. The letters were all too clear to me. *Beware M.* It was a warning and it was directed right at me.

Chapter Seven

SAINT MADELINE OF PROVIDENCE

May meant so many things that when it arrived I didn't know if I'd get through them all. For one thing, my ballet recital. For another, the announcement of who made the junior company of the Boston Ballet. On top of all that, it was First Communion Day at church. Although this was not something I personally had to do, or be involved in, the excitement around it at the Calabro house was contagious. I spent the entire afternoon there on the day of my ballet recital layering fried eggplants with mozzarella cheese and gravy, which is what they call red sauce, which is what my mother calls marinara. Then I raced from their house to the college auditorium where I would perform Spring for hundreds of people.

Antoinetta came, too, smelling of fried eggplants. Her father dropped her off and waited in the car. I could see her sitting alone from the wings, holding a little bouquet of carnations dyed blue. Secretly, I wished my mother would see Antoinetta and sit with her. But I also wished she wouldn't, because who knew what she might say or do that would be completely embarrassing.

Randy came up to me and said in his weird accent: "What are you?"

"Spring!" I said.

"Yes, Madeline, you are Spring. Be Spring. Be it!"

When he walked away, Demi Demilakis came up to me. She was all white and silver, for Winter, and she said, "Do you have a crush on him? Because people from Transylvania are vampires."

"He's not from Transylvania," I said. "He doesn't even know where Transylvania is."

Her eyes bulged out at me and she looked even weirder than usual because of the silver glitter all over her face.

"Where's he from, then?" she said.

"Estonia," I lied. That's where my father was. Estonia. He couldn't be at the recital because he was writing about Estonia for *National Geographic*.

Thinking about my father missing my performance made me sad, so I tried to think of spring things: tulips and baby birds and First Communions.

But Demi said, "Does your family want to come with my family for ice cream after?"

In one corner, all of the Summer ballerinas stood together in their pale blue costumes, their heads bent, their smiles radiant. Everywhere I looked, in fact, girls were helping one another pull their hair into buns, or sprinkle glitter on their cheeks. Demi and I were the outcasts. She looked so shimmery and hopeful standing there, but still I said, "Sorry. We already have plans."

"Maybe next time?" she said hopefully.

"Right."

The overture began, and Randy clapped his hands. "Places," he said in his mysterious accent. Maybe he was Estonian, I thought. I got into my line, the first one. I was Spring.

And I was magnificent. I could see my mother and Cody, both of them grinning and proud. I could see Antoinetta, impressed, maybe even dazzled not just by me, but by all of it. For a small moment, I actually felt happy. And it felt really, really good.

Holy Communion Day. The little girls wore white dresses and veils like brides, small crowns decorated with fake pearls and rhinestones, short white gloves. Some of them had a hint of pink lipstick on their lips, a splash of rouge on their cheeks, their hair twisted into French braids or buns high on their heads. They walked down the aisle of the church with a partner, a boy in a small navy blue suit and white shirt and bow tie. Two by two, in the same halting steps they would one day use when they got married. The boys' hair was parted, greased back, slicked down. They all looked terrified.

I squeezed Antoinetta's arm. "They're so lucky," I whispered.

But Antoinetta did not answer. She didn't talk in church. Especially not this church, Sacred Heart, the one her Aunt

Eleanor and Uncle Tootie attended. It was their daughter, Rachel, who was walking down the aisle now, her head held high beneath her fat bun and stiff veil. She clutched a small white cardboard purse with rosary beads and a picture of Jesus tucked inside.

I elbowed Antoinetta. "There she is," I whispered. Even though Antoinetta didn't answer, she smiled.

I watched Rachel as she continued down the aisle to her assigned pew. She kneeled deeply before she slid along the wooden bench and made a very precise Sign of the Cross. Only a couple years older than Cody, but little Rachel had such dignity. I sighed, too loudly, because now Antoinetta elbowed me and glared. But I didn't care. Not only was my poor brother being deprived of having a family that was not broken, but he was deprived of being a Catholic. Right then I wished I could pick him up and hug him tight. But all I could do was sigh again and have Antoinetta glare again and elbow me even harder.

Antoinetta had put on makeup: globby blue on her eyelids and two circles of blush on her cheeks. She had lipstick on her lips and dots of it on her front teeth. She tried to pull her hair into a chignon, but already strands had fallen loose, and her eyebrows looked even thicker and more like caterpillars with her hair off her face. Antoinetta always looked like a mess, even when she wasn't trying so hard to look good. She had two runs in one leg of her stockings and her skirt had twisted so that the zipper, which should have been on one side, was in the front. It was probably her sister's skirt, a hand-me-down, along with the mismatched jacket. Both were dark green, but different fabrics and shades. Her disheveled look made me love her even more.

I, on the other hand, had purposely dressed plain, in a sleeveless cotton dress with a cardigan to match. Still, Antoinetta's grandmother had frowned at me and muttered something in Italian, and Aunt Eleanor had tried to put lipstick on me, a scary shade of red. But I was only allowed to wear lip *gloss*, not lip*stick*, at least until I was thirteen. When I pointed out that I had lip gloss on, they all stared at my mouth and shook their heads. No matter how hard I tried, I would never fit into the Calabro family. But I didn't really care. Being around them was enough, standing in the kitchen on Sunday mornings while Mama Angie

fried sausage and Aunt Clara and Aunt Fanny smoked ciga-
rettes and pressed the tines of forks into dough to make
gnocchi.

The church bells started to ring and Antoinetta yanked
on my sweater, pulling me down to the kneeler. Content,
holy, saintlike, I knelt.

Antoinetta had told me that Aunt Eleanor thought she was
better than everybody. That's why she was having Rachel's
First Communion party at Wright's Chicken Farm instead
of at Mama Angie's, like everybody else always did.

"She's a big show-off," Antoinetta had said. But then
she added, "I don't care. I'd rather go to Wright's Farm,
wouldn't you?"

I shrugged. "I don't know what it is."

Antoinetta had given one of her really big laughs, the kind
that sounded like a donkey hee-hawing. "You've never eaten
at Wright's Farm?" she finally managed to say, before she
started laughing all over again. "Where does your family go
for special?"

"If my mother just doesn't feel like cooking we either go
to Minerva's for pizza or Hot Pockets for falafels. If it's

Cody's special night we go to China Inn for pupu platters. If it's my special night I don't care where we eat as long as we go to Pastiche for dessert, and I always get Key lime pie. And my mother makes us go to Al Forno to celebrate her special things, but we have to go at five and sit in the bar area so we don't bother the serious diners."

Antoinetta shook her head. "Well," she said, "you don't know what you're missing. Do you get the ziti at Al Forno? Big platters of it?"

"No."

"Just wait," Antoinetta had said.

Now we were inside Mr. Calabro's big Oldsmobile on our way to Wright's Chicken Farm. He was going to wait in the car while we all went inside and celebrated Rachel's First Communion. He wouldn't let that big show-off Aunt Eleanor pay for his meal, and also, Antoinetta had explained as we left the church, he didn't like parties very much since her mother died.

Antoinetta was talking about Johnny Depp; she had seen the movie *Pirates of the Caribbean* forty-seven times. But I wasn't listening. I'd already explained to Antoinetta that I thought Johnny Depp looked like a girl. Still, I let her keep talking about his girly face because I knew that eventually she would get around to something Catholic to talk about — she always did.

Until then, I was happy to think about all those little girls dressed like brides, how solemnly they'd knelt at the altar to receive the Communion wafer. You couldn't chew it, Antoinetta had explained. That would be like chewing Jesus's body up. You just had to let it dissolve on your tongue.

"Who's your patron saint?" Antoinetta asked all of a sudden, done with her Johnny rant.

I smiled. Boy, did I have Antoinetta figured out. "Maybe Saint Agatha?" I said.

Antoinetta looked horrified. "You don't want her," she said. "She's for breast cancer. That's too creepy."

"Who's yours?" I asked her.

"Saint Teresa. The Little Flower."

From the front seat, Antoinetta's father snorted.

"Pop hates her because she's French," Antoinetta explained. "But I don't care. She was so beautiful and young. All three of her sisters were nuns." Then she added, "She died of tuberculosis."

"Like Bernadette!" I said. "Maybe I should choose Bernadette as my patron saint?"

I thought of Jennifer Jones in the movie *The Song of Bernadette*. I had seen it in New York, and then I'd made my father rent it on video about a hundred times. "She was so beautiful, too," I said.

Antoinetta's father snorted again. She leaned forward and tickled the back of his neck with her fingertips. He swatted her hand away, but he was smiling. I could see him really clear in the mirror. I thought of my own father, who was so handsome and young. He had so many things Mr. Calabro didn't. Hair, for one. Nice teeth, for another. I would hate to have a father like Mr. Calabro, someone who always sat in his car and almost never talked.

Antoinetta leaned close to me. "He's been talking about your mother," she whispered.

"What?" I said, shocked and maybe even disgusted a little.

Antoinetta nodded. "He thought she was a knockout."

"What are you whispering about back there?" Mr. Calabro said.

"After the dinner," Antoinetta said, "we're going to Saint

Teresa's shrine, right, Pop? You promised. I was just telling Madeline."

"Yeah, yeah," Mr. Calabro said.

"We always go after Wright's Chicken Farm," Antoinetta said, winking at me.

Wright's Chicken Farm was big and noisy. Out front in a cage were chickens, as if to prove that their chickens were that fresh. All the food came in big platters. Salad and ziti with red sauce and then the chicken and French fries. I could hardly eat it all, but Antoinetta's relatives kept asking for the platters to be refilled.

"You eat like a bird," Aunt Fanny said to me, without even looking up from the chicken leg she was eating right down to the bone.

Finally, they were finished. The aunts went shopping in the gift store attached to the restaurant and the uncles took the little kids to see the chickens in the cages out front.

"Is Al Forno this good?" Antoinetta asked. But I knew it was just another rhetorical question.

As soon as we were done eating, Antoinetta asked her dad to take us to Saint Teresa's shrine. It was right down the street from the restaurant. Mr. Calabro led us to the car and we drove in silence.

"Go ahead," he said, turning off the engine. "Don't take all day."

"Doesn't he get bored in there?" I asked Antoinetta as we made our way across the gravel parking lot.

She shrugged. "Sometimes he keeps the car running and listens to talk radio."

I followed Antoinetta up a small hill where the statue of Saint Teresa stood.

"Isn't she beautiful?" Antoinetta said in a hushed voice.

She clasped her hands and fell to her knees before I could answer. My admiration of Antoinetta's reverence was endless. I dropped to my knees beside her, and stared up into the white stone face of The Little Flower.

"What did she do?" I said, making sure to keep my voice low. "You know, to become a saint?"

"Miracles," Antoinetta said. "Thousands. Maybe even millions. They say that in France, in Lisieux, there are offerings from around the world, Brazil and Alaska and China."

I studied Antoinetta's face. Even with the rouge and blue eyeshadow, she was so open, so pure, I couldn't help myself. I had to tell her. "I performed a miracle."

Immediately Antoinetta's face clouded.

But I didn't give her time to doubt me. I grabbed her arm and held it tight. "I've never told anyone before but I know you'll understand. It was when my mother and father were still married and we were all happy. My father went off on an assignment, to Idaho, and he was in an avalanche. Except none of us knew that. But the morning it happened, a voice called to me and told me he was in danger and I went alone to church and prayed all day." I had begun slow and hesitant but now a torrent, a waterfall of words, spilled out of my mouth. "And when I got back he was saved. A miracle. Right? A bona fide miracle."

I waited. I didn't know what I had expected. Questions, definitely. A demand for details. Or a rush of emotion. But not this nothingness. Antoinetta did not move. She hardly seemed to blink or breathe. In the distance, a horn sounded, a long blare.

"My father," Antoinetta said, though she did not get up.

"Before that," I added, feeling desperate, "I made a glass of water slide across our kitchen table just by concentrating."

"When your father got back, he left your mother, right?"

I nodded.

"So why the miracle, then? You saved him and he ruined your life. Everyone's life."

"No, no," I said. "He didn't. My mother did. She's awful with her stupid column and her boring clothes and the way she carried on, crying and hysterical. Maybe he would have come back if she'd only been different."

"Did you pray for that?" Antoinetta asked me. "Did you pray for him to come back?"

"At first. But not in the same . . ." — I searched for the right word, all the new vocabulary pushing through my brain — "*fervent* way that I did that day of the avalanche."

Again, the horn blared, longer this time.

"Do you know what I pray to Saint Teresa for?" Antoinetta asked.

I shrugged.

"A mother," Antoinetta said.

* * *

That night Antoinetta called me at home. She had never called me before. Her father didn't like her to talk on the telephone.

So when my mother came into the family room where I was looking up Saint Teresa in the encyclopedia — Saint Teresa of Lisieux; b. 1873, d. 1897 — and said, "It's Antoinetta," I was surprised.

I went into the kitchen to pick up the phone before she could answer.

"Hi," Antoinetta said. Her voice sounded all worried.

My mother came in, making all sorts of noise, and started to cook garlic in some olive oil on the stove.

"Hold on," I said. "It's very noisy in here."

I stretched the phone cord as far as I could so that I could stand around the corner in one of the kitchen's pantries. This one still smelled of the Greer's old dog's pee. No matter what we did, in warm weather the smell came back. When I passed my mother, the cord bumping into the edge of the stove, I gave her a dirty look.

"It is so hard to have privacy around here," I told Antoinetta loudly.

"Yeah, well," Antoinetta said, groping for something. Maybe she had called to apologize. She hadn't said one word in the car, just sat with her arms folded and stared out the window, ignoring me.

"So what's up?" I said. I was the one who should be angry. Antoinetta was the only person in the world who knew about my miracle and she'd acted like it was nothing, a waste of a miracle, really.

"I've been thinking. You know, about what you told me."

I glanced around the corner at my mother, who was adding chopped tomatoes to the pan.

"About my miracle?" I said, watching my mother, who was clearly eavesdropping on me, stirring the tomatoes.

"Yes," Antoinetta said. "All of a sudden it hit me. I was doing my homework and I thought, Madeline saved her father's life. It hit me just like that. And here's what I think. I think you should perform another miracle."

For an instant I was afraid that Antoinetta was going to ask me to bring back her mother. But Antoinetta was already saying, "I mean, you could be a saint, Madeline. You have to start being good, living a good life. You have to open yourself to the possibility of more miracles."

Antoinetta began to list all the things that could happen if I indeed became a saint. There was stigmata, where I would spontaneously bleed in the very spots where Jesus had been nailed to the cross.

"I don't want that one," I said, suddenly afraid of sainthood.

"There's the scent of roses, where you just emit the smell of roses for no earthly reason."

"You mean everywhere I went I would smell of roses?" I asked, imagining it. People's heads would turn. They would close their eyes and inhale deeply whenever I walked by. That one sounded better.

"There's bilocation," Antoinetta said. Now she sounded excited. "Like Padre Pio."

"Bilocation," I repeated. My mother's eyes flickered over to me, then quickly back down. "That's the one I want."

With bilocation, I could be in two places at once. I could be here with my mother and simultaneously be in New York City, living an important life with my father and Ava Pomme. On Friday nights, while Cody and I ate our mother's disgusting experimental dinners, I could bilocate and be at the Odeon, the coolest restaurant ever, in New York with my father, eating roast chicken and the best French fries in the world. They called them *frites*. And they were better than Wright's Chicken Farm.

I rolled the word *bilocation* around in my mouth.

Antoinetta was talking about other saintly virtues. Mom was draining the pasta in a colander in the sink, saying, "Time to eat, Madeline. Tell your friend you can call her later." Cody was walking into the kitchen, dragging a blanket I had not seen for years, the old worn-out baby blanket he used to carry with him everywhere until our mother hid it from him. "Not that again, Cody," Mom was saying. Antoinetta kept talking, her voice growing more and more excited with each possibility.

But I had just one thought and kept repeating it in my mind: *Saint Madeline of Providence*. That thought rendered me speechless.

"All right," my mother was saying. "You can keep it in the house but I am not lugging that ratty thing everywhere we go. Cody? Do you hear me?"

The steam from the pasta rose, enveloping my mother's

face so that she grew momentarily blurry. "Madeline? Now?"

"Visions," Antoinetta was saying. "Prophecy."

It felt like every single person was focused on me, Madeline, and I smiled happily, beatifically, thinking, *Saint Madeline of Providence.*

Chapter Eight

ITALIA

A week before we left for Italy, I waited next to the phone for the junior company of the Boston Ballet to call. Finally the phone rang and I saw the caller ID: Boston Ballet Company. *I got in!* They would only call if we were accepted, they had said.

"This is Madeline Vandermeer," I said when I answered, "and I am honored to accept this. Honored. Honored."

The woman on the other end was laughing by the second *honored.* But then I started to cry and she said, "Congratulations, Madeline."

Even though my parents were still divorced and my mother was still ordinary and all of the other terrible things in my life, I felt happy. Ecstatic, even. I thought about the patron saint of air travel, and how he used to levitate and float. That is how I felt that day.

And then, before I knew it, my mother and Cody and I were on an Alitalia 747 heading to Italy and I really was levitated, high above the Earth and everything I knew. Despite myself, I was excited, and I squeezed my mother's hand and even let her lift my hand to her lips and kiss me. Things were starting to change. I could feel it. By the time we settled into our hotel room, I was certain. Change was in the air.

For one, Italy changed Cody. It was as if he belonged there more than anyone else, as if Providence had been a temporary place for him to stay while he waited to come here. I noticed it and I was jealous, even though envy didn't become saints. I struggled with jet lag, waking at one or two every morning, unable to fall back asleep while Cody slept soundly through the night. When he woke up, he had energy, ready for everything and anything. He happily picked up the phone and ordered room service: caffè latte for our mother, blood-orange juice for all three of us, a tray of these crusty cream-filled pastries called *sfogliatelle*.

When the waiter arrived with the cart that bumped noisily across the floor, Cody was already showered and wrapped in one of the hotel bathrobes. But I could hardly pull myself out of bed after so many hours awake in the middle of the night, staring out the window, past the balcony, to the street beyond, where lovers rode their Vespas up and down, the girls holding on tight as the boys drove fast along the bay. Naples was noisy all the time, even at night. I was miserable, bleary-eyed, cotton-headed, homesick, even.

"How do you know that blood-orange juice isn't made from real blood?" I asked Cody. "Like monster blood?" I added.

This was the type of question that would have sent him into a fit of tears at home.

But here, in Italy, in Naples, it delighted him.

"Blah," he said, sticking out his tongue in the glass and lapping up some juice, "I've come to suck your blood."

He loved the food that Mom made us try. She always scribbled in her little notebook, sniffing things, asking our opinion, drawing little pictures. The stuffed and fried rice balls called *arancini*, and *calamari*, which was squid, and rolled meat stuffed with breadcrumbs and nuts and cheese called *brasciola*, he liked it all, while I stuck to pizza. Here, it was so wet I couldn't even lift it, even though that's what they expected you to do.

In between eating we took tours. We went up the funicular to Vomero and my mother let me choose a cameo, a small pin with a saintly face carved in ivory. "She looks like you," Mom said, and even though it wasn't true, I felt special and maybe even pretty. We spent a hot afternoon in the Archeological Museum, room after room of ancient treasures. Many of them had been plucked from Pompeii, put there for safekeeping from vandals and tourists eager for a souvenir ruin. Even though I grew fascinated by all the broken things there, the pottery shards and cracked columns and bits of people's lives, I got tired. Exhausted. Keeping my eyes open was almost impossible. Cody, on the other hand, chatted with the guards and made Mom read him descriptions of pottery and busts and sculptures of gods.

Italy also changed my mother. She transformed into someone new before my eyes, a worldly woman who could speak a few phrases in Italian, order in restaurants, negotiate prices with shopkeepers and cab drivers. She walked with great confidence. She even looked beautiful to me again. She and Cody walked ahead of me, pointing and laughing and taking pictures, while I dragged behind them.

"I am so unhappy," I would call to them. "I am so tired."

"Come on, slowpoke," they would call back.

How could a future saint be so tired in Italy?

Our next stop was Pompeii.

It was clogged with tourists, mostly German. Tour guides carried different colored umbrellas so their groups wouldn't follow the wrong leader. There weren't any English guides, so our mother bought a small book at the kiosks in front and we walked through the ruins together, Mom looking things up in the book as we went.

"The bakery," she said, reading from the guidebook, and there we saw the ovens, the two-thousand-year-old loaves of bread encased in volcanic ash, the bricks they used to heat them.

We found the Temple of Jupiter, the mayor's house, the amphitheater. The streets had deep ruts from the wheels of the chariots.

"Look," Mom said, pointing. "A one-way street."

All the ruts on the one-way street were on one side; the street that intersected it had them on the other side. It was incredible to see.

We ate the picnic our mother had packed on a grassy area near a small theater. Salami, cheese, olives, bread, and *limonata*, the lemon soda I like so much. *Limonata*, such a funny name. I suddenly started to feel less tired, less overwhelmed.

"Tomorrow can we go to some churches?" I asked my mother.

"All day. Every church in Naples," she said.

Always, behind us or looming ahead, no matter which way we turned, stood Mount Vesuvius. Its top was not pointed like other mountains; instead it was heart-shaped.

"That top," Mom explained, "blew right off."

I was amazed. Life had been ruined and then recovered in this place.

"Exhilarating, isn't it?" Mom said. "It's hard for you to understand what it's like when you feel like your life has been destroyed. I know this place might seem sad to some people, but to me it feels hopeful."

"Hopeful?" I said. "You ruined all of our lives and now all of a sudden a volcano makes you feel hopeful?"

I couldn't believe I had said it. I didn't know where it came from.

Immediately, I felt bad. The way my mother's face

collapsed, the way I could tell she was fighting back tears. Right when we were actually getting along.

"Is that what you think?" she asked finally. "That I ruined everything?"

I shrugged. "I don't know," I mumbled.

"That *is* what you think," she said, as if she had just realized that all my scorn for her was actually based on something.

I waited for her to prove otherwise. But of course she couldn't. Everything I knew to be true was true. My mother just sat there, staring.

Later, when she went to the trash can to throw out the remains of our lunch, Cody said, "How could you choose Ava over Mommy?"

"No one's choosing," I said. "We have them both."

"Well, lucky us," Cody said.

He ran to our mother and took her hand. I walked a few feet behind them, not because I was so tired anymore, but on purpose.

Saints had to suffer. I knew that and I knew I was really suffering. I was sick of being torn like this, of always having to take sides, even if it was only in my heart. I didn't know how to love each of my parents the same. More than anything, I wished I could go back and somehow make a different miracle. Of course I wanted my father saved. But maybe if there had been no avalanche at all, things would have stayed the way they were.

I had managed two miracles. If I could find another one, I could change things and be noticed. I lay in bed in the hotel in Naples, listening to the motorcycles whizzing past, the sounds of people having fun. Sometimes I even wished, in a very secret place, that my parents would get back together. I knew it was ridiculous. Why would Dad come back to his old boring life in Providence? And what would happen to Ava and Zoe if my father left them? And even if he did, with them in his life, it wouldn't be the same as before. I knew better than to waste my prayers, the way Antoinetta did. Her dead mother wasn't coming back. And how was her father ever going to meet a new woman if he never even got out of the car?

No. I needed to pray for the right thing.

I got up and stood by the curtain that opened out to the balcony. Beyond it was the Bay of Naples, the island of Capri, Vesuvius. Tonight the moon was a crescent one, my favorite. Most people liked full moons. They even wrote songs about them. But I liked this tiny sliver moon, the moon that was hardly there. I let myself pretend that when I turned around, my mother wouldn't be alone in the other bed. Instead, my father would be there beside her.

I remembered what it used to be like to crawl into their bed early in the morning. I would have to squeeze to get between them because they slept so close. Like spoons, my father used to say. How could two people who slept like spoons, year after year, not even live together anymore? I felt hot tears spill out of my eyes and run down my cheeks. I swallowed hard, in gulps. That was one way I knew to stop tears. And even though I was wasting prayers on the impossible, I prayed:

"Dear God, please bring our father back to us. Please let him be here, like spoons, with my mother."

It was ridiculous and useless and impossible, but wasn't that what a miracle was, making the extraordinary, the impossible, happen?

I turned around.

The hotel bed, a queen-sized one with lots of pillows and a fluffy comforter, looked as vast as the ocean with my mother there, drifting in it alone. I went over to it and climbed in beside her, turning so my front was pressed against her back, shaping myself into my mother's form. Without waking up, she felt me there instinctively and snuggled close. Then I closed my eyes, and filled with disappointment and confusion and faithlessness, slept.

We saw so many churches the next day that their names blurred. There was the big one where San Gennaro's blood liquefied every September; the one with the beautiful chipped tiles everywhere, leading out of the neglected garden; the modern-looking one where people went to get healed. And then there was the one in the old section of the city, across the crooked cobblestone street where the nativity figures were made.

Mom decided we should buy an elaborate nativity scene, with a big straw-covered manger and all the carved figures. She spent forever choosing the right Joseph and Mary, the perfect-sized archangels and wise men. Cody picked out funny figures to add: a winemaker, a butcher, a pizza man, a clown. The shop smelled bad, like cats, so after I picked out a fat baby Jesus, I stood in the doorway to get fresh air. But I watched Mom carefully. Ever since what happened in Pompeii, she looked different to me. Maybe because I knew I had hurt her in some deep, horrible way. I tried thinking mean thoughts, like *The truth hurts* and things like that, but it didn't make me feel better. Mom was hurt and I didn't know how to make it better.

The man who ran the shop flirted with her. He was younger than her, and he had a big blue birthmark on his cheek that I stared at. He caught me looking, and his fingers caressed the spot tenderly, as if to erase my gaze. I wondered how it would feel to live with something like that. And then I thought about divorce and how, in a strange way, it was like having something big, blue, and ugly. Divorce made you feel different than most people with real families. It made you uncomfortable.

"Can we take a taxi back?" Cody asked when we left. "I want to get back to the hotel and unwrap all the people we bought and play with them."

"I want to go in that church," I said, pointing at a gorgeous, old building.

I knew nothing about it. But I noticed it while I was standing in the doorway of the shop and even though we had been to enough churches already, I felt pulled toward this one.

"No!" Cody said. "I am so tired of churches!"

My mother looked at me tenderly. "I think we can stand one more, can't we, buddy?"

I ran across the piazza, feeling as if the church might hold some secrets. Inside, it was small and dark and empty.

My mother paid some euros for a guidebook and she and Cody walked around, trying to find what was described in it. Every church had some piece of famous art, a relic from a saint, an interesting apse or altar piece or ceiling.

But I went straight to the front, to the altar, and knelt. My whole body filled with the faint smell of incense and candle wax. I wanted another miracle. I wanted to be Saint Madeline of Providence. I prayed so hard that I didn't realize someone had come to kneel beside me.

It was a nun. A young, beautiful nun like Maria in *The Sound of Music*, and she had on a hat that looked like a paper airplane.

"*Americana?*" the nun said, not even bothering to whisper. When she spoke, I smelled roses, and I remembered that was one of the saintly qualities like bilocation that Antoinetta had told me about.

I nodded. I didn't like how everyone immediately recognized me as an American. Everywhere we went people knew.

"You pray hard, no?"

"Yes," I said.

I glanced around to be sure I could see my mother and Cody. They were staring into someone's tomb.

"You sad?"

I shrugged.

"You don't know?"

"No. I mean, yes, I do know."

"Ah," the nun said.

The nun began to pray, moving her lips silently.

I leaned in close to her to smell her rose smell. "I made a miracle," I whispered.

"Yes? That's very good," the nun said, unimpressed.

"If I make another one I'll become a saint. Saint Madeline of Providence."

"Ah." The nun shook her head. "No. First, to be a saint, you must be *morte*. Dead. Then you must wait a long time until someone remembers how good you were. Then they get together and talk about you and if you have a good miracle, maybe they beatify you. Then, after that, if you make another miracle, you be saint. *Basta*." The nun slapped her hands together like she was wiping something off them.

"But I saved my father's life," I said. I whispered the story to the nun, about the snow and the man's voice and the church. About the avalanche that changed our lives.

"Avalanche?" the nun said. "I don't know this word."

"It's when snow comes at you so fast that it ruins anything in its path. You don't know what hit you," I explained.

"Ah. I know it, yes. Avalanche." She touched my hand. "So now you try for a doubleheader, ha?" She laughed and it was like she was showering me with rose petals. "I like American baseball."

"I think if I pray hard enough I can make something happen. I'm just not sure what. Like last night, I was thinking that maybe my parents could get back together. But that's impossible."

"They divorce after the avalanche?" the nun said.

"Yes," I said, like something bad was caught in my throat.

"They funny things," the nun said. "Miracles. I no explain how your father survive avalanche or how you knew what you knew. This stays a mystery, eh? But I think miracles come from inside." The nun tapped her chest, hard enough for the wooden rosary beads she wore to quiver. "Then you feel like Saint Madeline of Providence, even if you not official saint.

Basta," she said, slapping her hands together again. "*Ciao,*
Santa Magdalena," the nun whispered.

I didn't want her to leave. For one thing, she definitely
knew more than Antoinetta, who had left out some major
milestones on the road to sainthood. For another, I felt like
she could look right into my heart.

Cody started calling to me, "Come on! Come on!"

"My brother," I said, turning to explain to my nun. But
she wasn't there. I looked around. She wasn't anywhere.
"Hello?" I said.

"Hello!" Cody whispered back, waving his arms like he
was parking an airplane.

When I still didn't budge, he came running to get me.

"Come on, already," he said. He tugged on my arm.

"Did you see that nun I was talking to?" I asked him.

"All I saw was some dead saint's ear. These relic things
are gross." I knew my mother had just taught him that word
and I smiled.

He tugged and he yanked, but I couldn't move. It was like
I was taking root, right there.

I inhaled. "Do you smell anything?" I asked him as the
faint scent of roses filled my nose.

"Yeah," Cody said. "I smell *church*."

Finally, all I smelled was church, too: incense and wax and stale air. My feet moved again, and I let Cody take me out of there.

After Naples and Capri we went to the Amalfi Coast and spent two nights in Ravello and four nights in Positano. The town, with its pastel-colored houses, hung from a cliff as if it might tumble at any moment. One of my vocabulary words rose up when I saw it: *precarious*.

"I hope we don't fall into the ocean," I told Cody when we first checked in, hoping to scare him. Now that my offical sainthood was further away than I'd thought, I could be bad again.

"That's silly," Cody giggled, disappointing me.

"Just as well that you guys are going to Rome," Mom said, trying to cheer herself up. "Tuscany is just vineyards and beautiful landscapes. Boring for you guys. You'll get to see the Colosseum and the Forum and the Trevi Fountain. And be sure to throw a coin in because that means you'll go back to Rome."

My heart swelled. I felt it getting bigger and bigger. My father was in Italy. We were all in Italy. I let myself imagine the four of us doing Italian things — twirling spaghetti and being a family.

"Is Daddy alone?" Cody said, narrowing his eyes. "Or with you-know-who?"

Mom pulled Cody onto her lap and buried her nose in his hair. "With you-know-who," she said.

I was getting used to switching parents. It no longer felt like stones in my chest. Now it felt like small dips, like the funny lurching feeling you get right before your roller coaster car takes a hill. Of course my father would be here with Ava Pomme and Zoe. They were a family. And I would be a part of that — for a while, anyway.

"I don't want to go to Rome," Cody said, and it was the first time since we got to Italy that he sounded like his whining old self. "I want to see beautiful scenery."

"Then look right over there," Mom said, pointing off in the distance.

I looked, too. It was impossible not to look. The beautiful sea glistening in the sunlight. The pastel houses. The tiled rooftops.

"I'm hungry," Mom said. "I think it's time for the beach and some lunch and some shopping. What do you say?"

My mother really was beautiful in Italy. The sunlight made her look soft and young. She'd bought a coral and turquoise necklace and she wore it every day. Against her tanned skin it seemed like an exotic and magical thing.

Our hotel was at the end of a steep road. When we left it to go to the beach, we had to navigate crowded streets as small as alleys, too small for cars to pass. Our mother bought pottery, mugs, and platters painted with brightly colored animals. I got a bathing suit and a pair of sandals.

Every afternoon we ate lunch at Bocca de Bucca on the beach, then we took our tatami mats and laid them on the pebbly sand. I collected sea glass. Some pieces were pottery shards, others were glass worn dull by the ocean.

While we sat on the beach, Mom told us again how lucky we were to go to Rome instead of on to Tuscany with her. But no matter how hard she tried, I could tell she was heartbroken.

On our last day in Positano, when we left the beach and went back to the hotel, a letter was waiting for me. I had left the addresses in Naples and Positano with Antoinetta, hoping she would find the time between Catholic day camp and babysitting her cousins to write me. I'd sent her dozens of postcards, of every church and the Blue Grotto and the piazza in Ravello. Of course I had sent postcards to everyone I could think of — Mai Mai Fan, who was in the Berkshires at some kind of genius camp; Sophie, who was on her grandparents' own island somewhere; even Bianca Plotz at her stupid summer camp in Maine.

Now, when the man behind the desk handed my mother the huge key with the long red tassel, he said, "And a letter for Signorina."

"Me?" I said, so happy I thought I might fly up the long marble stairs.

I didn't open it until after we got in the room and a waiter had delivered two limonatas and one Campari and soda. The three of us sat out on the balcony overlooking the houses clinging to the cliff above them, and the blue bay sparkling below.

"It's from Antoinetta," I announced.

"How nice," Mom said sadly, sounding like she missed us already.

The letter was written on old lady stationery, perfumed and flowery.

"Dear Madeline," I read out loud. "Thank you for the beautiful postcards of San Gennaro's and all of the other churches, too. Did you see San Gennaro's blood liquefy? You didn't happen to mention that. I am having a nice summer. I have watched some of those old black-and-white movies you told me about and I'm sorry to say I thought they were all really boring. Sorry."

I stopped reading long enough to roll my eyes, then I continued. "I wanted to tell you that my miracle came true, too." That made me stop reading out loud. I got up and walked into the room and continued to read:

"One day when my father and I went to the cemetery to put flowers on my mother's grave, we met a woman putting flowers on her husband's grave, one row away. We all said hello, to be polite. But my father and this woman, Connie Pietro, started to talk. Her husband died of an aneurysm which is really terrible because one minute you're fine and then you get a headache and boom! You're dead. At least we had time to prepare. Not Connie. And she's not very old either. Maybe thirty-five?

"Anyway, that was just three weeks ago, right when you left, and you're not going to believe it but they are getting married in September! Do you know what she said to me yesterday when we all went to Wright's Chicken Farm to celebrate? She said, 'Antoinetta, I hope after we get married you'll be able to call me Mom.' Saint Teresa heard my prayers, Madeline. I have to go and make her an offering of thanks. Maybe I'll wait until you get back home.

"Love from your friend,

"Antoinetta Calabro.

"P.S. I hope this news won't be a disappointment to your mother?"

"What happened?" my mother called to me. I walked back onto the balcony.

"Her father's getting married," I said, still not quite believing it myself.

"Who would want to marry that funny little man?" my mother said.

"They met in the cemetery," I explained.

"Creepy," Cody said. "What are they, vampires?"

"It's a miracle," I said, folding up the letter and putting it back in the envelope.

Chapter Nine

WHAT I KNEW

As soon as Cody and I got to Rome, I knew one thing right away: Ava Pomme wanted *her* family to be in Rome, not my family. In New York, we were always just passing through. But this time was different. We had big duffel bags, bulging backpacks, digital cameras. We settled in and it made Ava very unhappy. It was in the nervous way she moved around the hot, stuffy apartment, her hands fluttering oddly, her face pinched. The way she said to our father, "Why don't you take your kids to the park?" And, "Could you talk to your daughter about cleaning up after herself?" New lines had been drawn, I thought. And then I realized that maybe they weren't so new. Maybe I just never noticed before. Even Baby Zoe was crankier than usual, fussing all night in the stark, unfamiliar room where her crib, unlike the one she slept in back in New York, had no happy dangling creatures, no tiny Brahms lullaby playing. Sometimes, in the middle of the night, Zoe began to scream, a loud, shrill scream that woke everyone.

Ava said it had to do with learning to walk, which Zoe had done on their first day in Rome. She had stood, teetered, then, zombie-like, made her way across the floor. Day after day she'd picked up speed, and was now climbing onto chairs and beds, always seeming about to fall off at any moment. She scurried up the stairs, glancing behind her at the adults who chased after her. She stopped taking her regular morning naps and instead cried from exhaustion, falling every few steps but unwilling to stop.

On our second day in Rome, Ava hired Carmela, the old lady who lived on the first floor, to take Cody and Zoe to the Borghese Gardens. The moment they left, Ava locked herself in the bathroom and took a really long shower. She emerged from the bathroom, her hair wet, wearing a fluffy white bathrobe that made her look fat. Even though she smiled at me, her eyes had a bruised look about them and the corners of her mouth were pulled in tight. She didn't look very pretty lately. I thought of my mother in Positano, her coral necklace, the flowered scarf she bought that made her look like an old movie star. She had stopped using that weird hair stuff, too, and her hair had grown a tiny bit and she stuck it behind her ears, which was so much better than the electrocution look.

Thinking of Mom made me sad. All of a sudden I felt all the sadness I should have felt when my father first moved out and Mom used to cry all the time, over the least little thing. I had a terrible memory just then, one I had tried to forget: Once, just a couple of weeks after he left, Mom decided to bake a cake. It wasn't anybody's birthday or anything; she just wanted to bake a cake. Baking relaxed her, she always said. But she kept messing up. She couldn't remember whether she put in the baking powder or not. We were out of vanilla so she used almond extract instead. I sat in the kitchen watching her getting more and more upset at how she couldn't even bake a simple cake. It was one of the things she was good at and now she couldn't even do that. And every mistake she made started her crying again. When she took the eggs out of the fridge, she tripped over nothing at all, and dropped the whole dozen on the floor. She plopped down, right there in the middle of the kitchen, trying to pick up the long strands of yolk, the pool of goo slowly expanding, refusing to be caught. She cried, harder and harder, as she worked at those broken eggs. Now I wished I had tried to help, had done something. I thought about the way my mother felt during a hug, as if her whole body might just melt into mine. It sent a cozy warmth right through me.

Ava was making her coffee in the press pot, thick stuff that left black grounds in the bottom of the cup.

"Did you know that I'm the one who saved Dad?" I asked carefully.

"Saved him?" Ava said, without looking up.

She was too busy concentrating on getting the coffee right. Yesterday the whole thing had exploded in an eruption of boiling water and coffee grounds, spraying the floor and walls and Ava's white robe. I could still see some faded brown stains at the hem.

"Saved him how?" Ava said.

"In the avalanche," I told her. I don't know what made me tell my miracle to Ava Pomme. But she put down the coffee-pot and gave her full attention to me.

"That avalanche?" she said. "But you were at home. You were a little girl."

"No, I wasn't," I said, irritated. "I was ten." I added under my breath, "I wasn't little."

"I just mean I don't see how —"

"Forget it," I said.

Ava hesitated. She wasn't always sure what the right thing to do with kids was. That was one of the things that made her so appealing usually. She didn't know you weren't supposed to let kids stay up late or give them cappuccino, or a million other things. But all of a sudden, it seemed stupid for her to be so clueless about kids. For one thing, she had her own kid. For another, she was a grown-up.

Ava began to heat some milk for the coffee.

"Do you believe in miracles?" I asked her, studying Ava's back, her slim waist under the belted robe, the shape of her rear end. When I first met her, Ava was already pregnant with Zoe, a tall skinny woman with a ridiculously big belly.

"No," Ava said. She put her hands on her hips and stared into the pot of milk.

"How do you explain things like Saint Bernadette?"

"I saw the movie," Ava said, "but I can't really remember."

"Lourdes," I said, disgusted. Even my mother knew about these things.

"Right," Ava said. "All those sad people go there to drink the water —"

"Bathe in it."

"Okay. Bathe in it. Then they go home and die, anyway."

That picture of Antoinetta's mother flitted across my brain.

"Well," I said, uncertainly, "God has to agree that the person should be saved."

Ava laughed. "That hardly seems fair, does it?" She poured some milk into her cup, then added the coffee. When she sipped it she grimaced. "It's so hard to find good decaf coffee here."

"The thing is," I continued, "I asked God to spare my father. From that avalanche. And he did."

Ava studied my face harder than she ever had before. "You mean," she said finally, "you got the news of the avalanche and began to pray? And then the next thing you heard he was saved?" I could tell that she was thinking hard, carefully choosing her words. "Because, you know, by the time you heard about the avalanche he had been saved. We just didn't know that. The news didn't have reports of survivors yet, only news that there had been an avalanche. So you were praying but really, he was all right."

I wanted to explain better, about the voice and everything, but I couldn't. Ava's words had taken hold of something inside of me and squeezed it hard. She had said "we didn't know." But my father hadn't even known Ava yet. My family was the "we" then and Ava Pomme was not part of our family. All of that came after. After the avalanche, after he got back home. Then the arguments began and the word *divorce* floated around our house like a bad spirit. But now, I wasn't sure.

"Madeline?" Ava was saying. "Do you see what I mean?"

"I think so," I said softly, trying to put everything in the right order. If my father already knew Ava, maybe even knew her back when I had danced in *The Nutcracker*, then I had saved him only to have him leave all of us and go to Ava Pomme. The Ouija board's warning came back to me: *Beware*

M. Antoinetta had told me it was a sin to consult Ouija boards, tarot cards, or phone-in psychics. I didn't want to sin, but that Ouija board had sent me a warning. Maybe it was a warning about Ava Pomme.

"Now if you had prayed before the avalanche and then he lived, that would be different," Ava was saying, "but why would you do that?"

"But that's just it!" I blurted, forgetting for a moment what I was considering. "I didn't know about the avalanche. I got a message or something. A premonition, maybe, that Daddy was in trouble. And I ran to the church and I prayed and I prayed and when I got back, he was saved."

Ava stood, walked over to the sink, and emptied her coffee into it. "I'm sure there's a reasonable explanation," she said.

"Ava?" I said, taking a step closer to my stepmother. Funny, I hardly ever thought of Ava as that: stepmother. The word conjured toothless witches, people with bad intentions.

Ava sighed, bored with this conversation, or with me. It wouldn't be the first time. She often got impatient, like when I told a joke too many times or didn't understand something and asked for an explanation. For a mother, she sure didn't have any patience. With a sharp pang, I remembered how long my real mother spent teaching me to tie my shoes, to write my name. *M is for mountain,* she had taught me, *and it looks like a mountain.*

I was thinking all these mixed-up things and staring at Ava Pomme. Something flickered in her eyes, then went out. Just a brief shadow, but I saw it. Right then, I realized that if I was right, if I had figured this out, then so had my mother, probably a long time ago, back when it all first happened. And for two whole years my mother had let me hate her rather than telling me the truth and letting me hate my father. My mother had faith in us, and faith protected us from the truth. Somehow we would come back to her eventually.

The largeness of my mother's love made me breathless. I thought of that list she had made. The first thing she'd been grateful for was us: *The kids, of course.* Ava Pomme would never put me on a list of things to be grateful for, I was certain.

"Ava?" I said again.

"Hmmm?" Ava said, distracted, and trying once again to make a pot of coffee. I got the clear impression that a good cup of coffee was a lot more important than I was.

"When exactly did you know about the avalanche?" I asked.

"Why, it was all over the news," Ava said. "I think the whole country held their collective breath, waiting to hear if there were survivors." She busied herself with the coffee-pot. "Like when that little girl fell in the well. You probably don't remember that. Some little girl fell in a well in Texas and it took days to rescue her and everyone was waiting to hear if she was alive or whatever."

Ava glanced up at me.

"That was a close one," she said.

Carmela from downstairs smelled good, like the fresh rosemary that my mother cooked with. She had strange bumps on her face, smooth hills of flesh scattered everywhere, and one large brown spot on her cheek. Her face was like a village: The bumps were all the little houses, the brown spot an irregular-shaped lake, and the deep lines on her cheeks the roads and tributaries that led to other, more exotic and mysterious places. I wanted nothing more than to crawl into that face and explore it.

Carmela had come to watch Zoe so that everyone else could "have a meal in peace."

She called me Magdalena. But she did not know what to make of Zoe or Cody's names. Whenever she heard them, she clucked her tongue and shook her head. She didn't even try to pronounce them in her broken English. I liked to stare at Carmela. Her hair was stark white and long, pulled back in a complicated twist, held in place by long dark bobby pins. But I liked to imagine it free, billowing around her head in its snowy grandeur. The blue color of her eyes reminded me of ice, and she had a way of turning them onto something or someone as if they could bore through the surface and discover something important.

Reluctantly, I left Carmela behind, rocking Zoe easily to sleep so we could go eat dinner together.

"Amazing," Ava said as we started to leave, "she's been so fussy."

Carmela gave Ava a penetrating stare. "Yes," she said. She continued humming her seemingly random song, rocking and pressing her fingertips on the center of Zoe's forehead.

At the restaurant Ava said, "That woman gives me

the creeps. It was like she put a spell on Zoe. Did you see her?"

"Who cares?" my father said, leaning back in his chair, drinking his red wine. "It's the first time she's slept in weeks."

At this restaurant, a small crowded place with picnic-type tables, there were no menus. Instead, the waiter delivered whatever food the chef was cooking. He watched everyone who came in, made sure they were eating, shouted to them in Italian.

But when we came in he shouted, "Hey! *Americanos*? Want some Coca-Cola? Want some Pizza Hut?"

Even though he smiled when he said it, showing two shiny gold teeth, I felt embarrassed. Other families looked at us and laughed. *"Americano,"* someone at the next table whispered. I wished I looked interesting, like Carmela. I played with my hair, pulling it back and twisting it this way and that.

"Scott," Ava said, "tell her not to do that at the dinner table."

"Madeline?" Dad said obediently.

I didn't stop. I twisted my hair and thought about how Ava always did that. *Scott,* she'd say, *tell Madeline we have to leave. Scott, ask Madeline if she likes oysters.*

The waiter brought us two large, thin-crusted pizza margheritas.

"Scott," Ava said. "Her hair."

"Daddy," I said to my father, "tell Ava I'm done fixing my hair."

Cody sighed. "I love Italy," he said. "I want to live here forever." He leaned forward. "Have you ever noticed the cars here don't have airbags?" He leaned back again and took a big bite of pizza. "Yup," he said dreamily, "I could live here forever."

"It takes some getting used to," Ava said carefully to Dad. She saw me watching her and forced a smile. "Of course, I traveled through Asia a few years ago and loved it. Now, that was difficult. No roads to speak of, and you had to be so careful about what you ate. Not like Rome, where you can even drink the water from the tap."

The waiter brought the next course, spaghetti carbonara.

"Hey!" the chef called. "*Americanos!* Some Chef Boyardee, eh?"

"If only they made pasta this good," Dad answered him cheerfully.

"What is this?" Cody asked, leaning over his plate to sniff the spaghetti.

"Remember Mom made it once?" I said, breaking an unspoken rule to not speak of my mother in front of Dad and Ava. I didn't care. "It was a Friday night dinner and she called it bacon and egg spaghetti."

That same feeling of longing swept over me. If I could just hug my mother, I might feel better.

"Maybe we could call Mom tonight?" I asked my father.

"Sure," he said, keeping his attention on the spaghetti he was twirling around his fork. He kept twirling, absently, even after the strands were tightly wound.

"It's good," Cody said. "Better than Mom's."

"She probably didn't use pancetta," Ava said.

I looked at Ava sharply. "By the way," I said, "I was thinking about something."

"Shoot," Dad said.

"I was thinking about how I don't know the story of how you guys met. You know how I love romantic stories."

"Not so romantic," he said. "We met at a bar."

"It was romantic," Ava said, hurt.

"Well."

"But when?" I said, thinking about what Ava had said that morning: *We just didn't know then.*

"Well," he said again, "I had a meeting with an editor that ran late, so I was staying overnight and, luckily for me, I decided to have a drink."

Pleased with the "luckily for me" part, Ava smiled. "Lucky for both of us," she said.

"So this is a love story?" Cody said as he sucked spaghetti into his mouth.

"Of course it is, Cody," Ava said. "Now how would they say it in Italian? *La grande passione?*"

"I mean," I said, "when was this?"

"Let me see," my father said.

"I mean, it had to be after the avalanche. Because remember right before you left for Idaho, you and Mom and Cody came to see me in *The Nutcracker* and then we had dinner in Chinatown and you made a toast. You said, 'To the most wonderful family in the world. My funny son. My dancing daughter. And my wife, the woman I love.'"

My father cleared his throat.

"Then," I continued, "you went to Idaho and when you came home, you and Mom got a divorce."

"And you disappeared," Cody added softly.

"But later, Ava and I got married and we had Zoe and everything turned out fine."

Cody and I both stared at him.

"And now," our father said, "we have a different, wonderful family."

"I remember Boston," Cody said. "How we all used to stay in bed together on Sunday mornings and I could watch cartoons and I would squeeze in right between you and Mommy. You used to call it a Cody sandwich, remember?"

Dad nodded, but he looked kind of nervous.

"I liked the bottom," I said. "I liked to lay longways across the foot of the bed."

The waiter appeared again, with a platter of veal.

"Look at this," Ava said with more cheerfulness than anybody felt. "Now would this be a *piccata*?"

Under the table, I felt my brother's hand reach for mine. I took it. Sometimes I forgot Cody was really just a little kid. His hands felt so small and smooth.

Instead of eating the veal, which you weren't supposed to eat, anyway, because it was a baby calf who had been killed in some very horrible way, I stared at Ava. My stepmother. The more they didn't say, the clearer it became: My father had supposedly loved my mother. All of that was fake. I watched as Ava put a piece of veal in her mouth and pronounced it *delicioso*. Our mother would have cut some for Cody first, into bite-sized pieces. Our mother would have asked me why I wasn't eating any. She would have respected my knowledge about the whole veal thing.

I watched as Ava chewed and talked and smiled away.

"It's a baby, you know," I said. "A calf. And they chained it up and everything."

"Not here," Ava said. "They do everything differently here."

I didn't think that was true. Ava was smooth, the way she came up with the answers so easily. She had an answer for everything. I just kept watching her. I was, maybe, starting to hate Ava a little.

Carmela poured hot water in a bowl, added a few drops of olive oil, then waited, peering into the bowl.

"I think you maybe got the *mal occhio*, no? The Evil Eye?" Carmela said to Ava.

"No, really, it's just a headache. Too much wine, perhaps," Ava said.

"No," Carmela said, pointing to the bowl. "You got the *mal occhio*. I fix. No problem."

She took Ava's hand — which Ava gave her reluctantly — and made circles on the palm with her fingers, muttering to herself.

"Really," Ava said nervously. "It's just a headache. I have some ibuprofen."

"Someone maybe no like you?" Carmela said. "Or maybe you cross somebody?"

"Cross somebody?" Ava said, laughing. She rubbed her palm where Carmela had held it. "I don't think so. Of course, people are always offending others without meaning to."

"Offending?" Carmela asked.

Ava looked around for my father to come in the kitchen and rescue her, but he was on the telephone in the bedroom, with the door closed. When she caught my eye, I glared, trying to make an evil eye.

"You know, hurting someone's feelings," Ava explained.

"Ah. You do this?"

"I don't know," Ava said. "Maybe. Without meaning to."

"And now your headache, it's all gone?"

Ava's hand touched her temple lightly. "It is. Yes."

Carmela stood. She was a large woman, and she got to her feet slowly. She put on her handkerchief, a black silk one with red poppies on it, and picked up her black purse, its gold clasp gleaming in the light.

"So. You maybe be careful, eh? About who you offend?"

Ava laughed the same nervous laugh. "Really. It was more likely the cheap wine we had with dinner."

"Hmmm," Carmela said. "Good night, Magdalena." She pressed my cheeks with her fingers. "You a smart girl, eh? A good girl?"

I looked at Carmela's ice blue eyes. I thought of mountain tops, cool lakes.

Carmela nodded. Muttering, she walked out.

"God," Ava said, emptying the water and olive oil from the bowl and running hot water into it. "She gives me the creeps."

But she didn't give me the creeps at all. You know who was starting to give me the creeps? Ava Pomme.

Chapter Ten

HOME

A postcard arrived for me from my mother: a picture of Saint Catherine of Siena's head in its reliquary at the church of Saint Dominic in Siena.

"How ghoulish," Ava said, leaning over my shoulder to peek.

I slapped my hand over the postcard, hiding it from Ava. "Excuse me?" I said.

Ava came around to sit across from me.

"A head?" Ava said. "Not only is it positively ghoulish, but for a mother to send a postcard of such a thing to her daughter. Well."

I narrowed my eyes at Ava. What did this woman know about mothers and daughters, anyway? Now that her own daughter was turning into someone, Ava grew more baffled every day. Zoe screamed, "No!" at just about everything Ava gave to her: small perfect tortellini, plump purple figs, focaccia smeared with olive oil and salt. To all of it Zoe screamed, "No!," often sweeping it off the table with a grand gesture. Whenever she ate pasta in red sauce, Zoe dropped her face right into the bowl and gobbled it like a dog. Ava could only look on, horrified. It was my father who carried Zoe over to the sink and washed the sauce out of her hair and face and from in between her fingers. One of Ava's favorite things to say lately was, "Scott, do something."

I turned over the postcard and began to read the message. It was full of details of the churches in Siena, the monastery at La Verna, all the things she knew I would like.

"How is your mother?" Ava asked, trying to sound casual and uninterested.

I pretended I didn't hear her. My emotions, about Ava and my mother and everything, were all mixed up inside of me. I could feel them bubbling up like one of my mother's stews.

"Madeline?" Ava said.

I dropped the postcard into my lap. "I thought you weren't supposed to ask," I said.

"What do you mean?" Ava said.

"I mean," I said dramatically, "I thought you weren't supposed to ask about my mother. She's off limits, right?"

Ava made a nervous little sound in her throat. Back in New York she seemed confident and in charge. Here, she was a mess. She even looked shorter here.

"No one ever said that," Ava said.

"Fine," I said. "Then here's how she is. She has managed to take care of us and keep writing and run a house that is practically falling on our heads while Daddy ran off with you." My heart was beating fast. I was saying things that hadn't seemed to take shape yet in my head, but once I opened my mouth and the words began to spill out they made perfect sense. "Because that's what happened, isn't it? Daddy met you before the avalanche and left all of us for you. It's the only thing that makes sense."

Ava opened her mouth to speak, but no words came out. Footsteps came from down the long hallway that led to the bedrooms. My father was taking Zoe and Cody to the little park up the street, where there was a playground and ponies to ride.

"Madeline," Ava managed to say, but that was all. And really, what more could she say?

The kitchen door flew open and Cody ran in, followed by our father with Zoe on his shoulders.

"Everyone coming?" he asked.

It was as if I was seeing him for the very first time, someone who had been reckless with my heart, with all of our hearts, my mother's most importantly. I gulped and shook my head. Downstairs, I knew, old Carmela would be sitting by the window watching Rome go by. She would be sipping one of those terrible drinks she had for her indigestion, and eating stale bread.

"I'm going downstairs," I said, already moving away from them.

"Honestly, Scott," Ava said, "I don't know how she can stand that old woman."

I swung around to face Ava. "Well, then, you don't know anything about me, I guess."

I saw my father's look of surprise, and the way Ava's hand with its perfectly painted oval nails went to her mouth. But I turned my back on them and went downstairs.

Carmela toasted yesterday's bread and drizzled it with olive oil and salt. None of her plates matched, and her cups were chipped. But I didn't care. I loved her and her things and the way she looked suspiciously at Ava Pomme.

"She's not my real mother," I whispered as we watched Ava leave the house alone, a big black leather bag swung carelessly over her shoulder. Without any of us around she regained her New York self. Her hair looked shinier, and she walked with a certainty that she lost under the weight of family life.

"Your father marry younger woman, throw your mother away, eh?" Carmela said, nodding as if she'd known it all along.

"Yes," I said, realizing that was exactly what he had done. One of my vocabulary words came back to me. "He jettisoned us," I said.

Ava Pomme walked along the street, pausing to stare into the shop windows, until she finally disappeared from sight.

I wished it really was that easy, that by just staring at her she would vanish.

"I hate her," I sighed. What I knew was that Ava Pomme was not going to vanish anytime soon, no matter how hard I stared.

"Me, too," Carmela agreed. "She bossy and she stupid."

We looked at each other and laughed like conspirators.

"Well," I said, " my mother comes tomorrow to get us and take us home." I added, "I can't wait to see her."

Suddenly, I felt an ache for my mother that was so enormous I almost fell over. I pictured her in our backyard, working in the sunless garden there. I saw her at the stove, sprinkling herbs, tasting, and correcting. If I closed my eyes, I could almost feel the shape of her that night in Naples, her strong shoulders, her hair that smelled of generic-brand strawberry shampoo.

Ava went to a fancy drugstore in Greenwich Village and bought tubes and bottles of expensive toiletries. I liked to go into Ava's bathroom and take all of the lids off everything and inhale their exotic smells. But now I longed for my mother's simple smell of Ivory soap or no-name toothpaste. I remembered complaining not too long ago about the cheap stuff, holding up a bottle of fancy shampoo, and the way my mother had taken the other kind and read off the ingredients, making me compare. "How embarrassing!" I had shouted. "How cheap!" And then I'd buried my face in the racks of magazines, leaving her to do all of the shopping herself.

"I miss my mother," I said, and that ache grew so great that the only way to relieve it was to cry.

"Oh," Carmela said, patting her ample lap, "come here, *cara mia*. Come here."

I climbed onto the old woman's lap and let her wrap her arms around me. They did not feel like my mother's arms, knowing and familiar, but they held the comfort of someone who understood a broken heart.

That night, my father told me to dress up fancy — the two of us were going on a date.

"I don't want to," I said miserably. All I wanted was to go to bed and sleep until my mother came for us. Then I would hug her and not let go. I would tell her how sorry I was for every bad thought I'd had, every cross word, all of it. I would tell her she was a good mother, the best mother ever.

"But you have to," my father was saying. "You and I need a proper celebration for your acceptance to the Boston Ballet School. We're going to dinner at a restaurant near Piazza Navona, and then we'll get ice cream later."

I loved ice cream in Rome, with all the flavors I had never tasted before, chestnut and hazelnut and zabaglione. I loved the Piazza Navona, too, with its fountain lined with statues hiding their eyes. My mother had said that the sculptor for the fountain, angry that he had not been commissioned to build the church as well, made the statues cover their eyes from the church's ugliness. My father said that story was not true; the dates when each had been built proved the falseness of that tale. But I didn't care. I chose to believe my mother's version.

Dressing, I struggled to remember things my parents had agreed on. But I could find none. Those happy times of just a few years ago were already fading away. They couldn't even agree to stay married, and now I knew why.

Cody tiptoed in, his eyes wide. "Don't leave me with her," he said.

We were united now in our hatred of Ava Pomme, home-wrecker, wicked stepmother, *strega* — witch.

I shrugged. "I think Daddy's trying to cheer me up."

"But she'll ignore me all night. I'll have to color or something."

Cody hated to color, but Ava had bought him dozens of coloring books and crayons because she never bothered to notice how much they bored him.

"Can't you stay in the lines?" he mimicked. *"Why is the girl's face purple?"*

I laughed. *"Strega,"* I whispered.

"Strega," Cody whispered back.

The cafes in the piazza were full in the warm summer night. People sipped coffee and emptied liters of wine, their heads bent together in conversation, cigarette smoke furling around them.

"Cody loves Italy," my father said.

He had his arm hooked in mine, so gentlemanly that I could almost, but not quite, forget that he was not a gentleman. Gentlemen followed certain rules of behavior, and even though I wasn't certain exactly what those rules were, I knew they didn't include cheating on your wife or jettisoning your family. He guided me to an outdoor table, pulled out a chair for me to sit, then pushed it back in, effortlessly.

"How about you?" he asked when he settled himself into the seat across from me. "How do you like Italy?"

I wanted to explain the things I loved here, the churches and the oldness and the way the Italians understood something important about me. But wrapped up in that was what I had figured out here, about him and Ava Pomme. I felt homesick. I missed my mother. I didn't know how to say all of that, how to tell my father that I thought Italy was wonderful but he was not. A part of me still loved him so much that I wished what I knew could go away.

"It's all right, I guess," I managed to say. It was the best I could do.

He looked surprised. "I figured you loved it, Mad," he said. "What with your interest in religion and your love of churches and saints."

Mad. Funny that my little girl nickname expressed exactly how I felt. Why couldn't my father see that?

The waiter came over and my father ordered wine and food in perfect Italian. Every morning he went off to Italian class. That's how he was, total immersion with everything new. If

I bothered to ask him, he could tell me the dates of Roman war victories, who had built which building and when. He could quote what Henry James had to say about Rome, and what was written on Shelley's grave over in the Protestant cemetery. He could teach me to conjugate verbs.

When the waiter brought our wine, my father poured a little in a glass for me. I thought about how happy this would have made me just a few days ago. Now, it just added to my misery.

"When in Rome," he said, and even though he didn't have to finish the old saying, he did, maybe just to fill up the empty space between us, "do as the Romans do."

I folded my arms across my chest and made him work hard at a conversation.

He'd ordered all of my favorite things, buffalo mozzarella with basil and tomatoes, a pizza with *quattro formaggio*, gnocchi in tomato sauce.

"To my prima ballerina!" my father said, lifting his glass.

I was expected to clink mine against his, to smile and adore him. But I did none of these things. Instead, I said, "Remember when I asked you if I could live with you and

Ava? In the spring, when Mom told me I couldn't study with Madame anymore?"

Slowly, my father lowered his glass, which was suspended there in midair while I talked.

"Remember you said no?"

My father took a quick sip of his wine. He sat up straight. "When you were a little girl," he said, "I used to make you promise that when you got older you wouldn't act like a teenager. That you wouldn't grow obstinate or argumentative. That you would stay your wonderful self."

"I am my wonderful self," I said.

He laughed and said, "Yes! You are! You made the cut for that school. How many kids tried out, Mad? And how many got picked? Bravo!"

I frowned. My insides were getting all jumbled up. I always loved the way my father had of making me feel special. It was hard to reconcile that with the fact that he was a cheater and an abandoner.

"Speaking of wonderful," he was saying, "Ava and I have some wonderful news."

My mouth tasted sour, like I might throw up. "I have

a terrific new book contract on investigating the church's practice of canonization, and Ava and I are going to live here for a few years. Right in Rome. We've rented a big apartment near the Pyramid so that when you and Cody come to visit next summer there will be plenty of room."

"You mean I'm not going to see you until next summer?" I said. That cheese was rising up in my throat, all four kinds, and I had to swallow hard to keep it where it belonged.

"Living in Europe is an incredible experience that I want my children to have," he said. "It's a once-in-a-lifetime opportunity, really."

Once in a lifetime. That was the same thing my mother had said when she'd tried to convince me to come on this trip. Was that what adults really believed, that opportunities only came once in a lifetime? I couldn't imagine that in my entire life that stretched before me that I would never again visit Italy if I wanted to, or never get the chance to live in a different country. But it seemed that adults forgot about possibility, that in a life there were always new chances to take, new roads to travel. How sad grown-ups seemed to me at that moment, with their vision of lost opportunities and missed chances.

I was folding my pale pink napkin into small accordion

pleats, tight ones that would spring open if I let them go. But I didn't. I held them tight.

"But I won't be living here. Only Zoe and Ava and you will be. I'll be a whole continent away." My stomach churned some more. I had wanted to jettison my father, but here he was, casting me off again.

"Madeline, you're going to have an amazing year with ballet and everything. Then you'll spend next summer in Italy with us. And," he added, "guess what?"

I didn't guess.

"You're getting another brother or sister."

"What?" I said, jumping to my feet.

"Ava and I are having another baby. Due on New Year's Day. The start of a great year, right?"

I couldn't believe what I was hearing. How could he think that this was going to make me happy, watching his life fall into place while the rest of us tried to fix our own?

"For you and your real family, maybe," I said. "You ruined my life once by falling in love with Ava Pomme while you were supposed to be loving us — taking care of us. And for all this time I've been on your side when really I should have been on Mommy's. There you were buying a new house and telling us how wonderful we were when you were doing what? Secretly meeting Ava Pomme? And leaving Mom with all the broken things? And now you're moving to Rome and leaving me!"

Conversation around us came to a halt, except the whispered *Americano*, the embarrassed glances away from us.

I made sure everyone was still listening when I shouted, "I hate you!"

Then I threw up, all over the gnocchi and the pretty pink tablecloth. I had not thrown up since I was a little kid, and it felt awful. I ran out of the café, fast, across the piazza where lovers nestled each other and small children chased one another, squealing with joy. I ran past the fountain, where the statues and their covered eyes seemed meant for me. I ran up the stairs of the church and through its open doors. Inside, it was hushed and dark, except the candles flickering in their tall red chimneys.

I kept running, down the aisle to the altar. When I reached it I dropped to my knees on the cool marble floor, clasped my hands together, bent my head, and prayed for a miracle.

I did not know how long I stayed there like that. But as I knelt and prayed, a vision played out in my mind. It was my life, really, the one that before the divorce stretched out in front of me with so much hope and possibility. I didn't realize that all this time I had wanted the impossible to happen, just like Antoinetta. But now I saw that. I thought of all the times in my life, ballet recitals and performances, graduations and proms, even my wedding and the birth of my own children, all of these times when a person's parents came together to celebrate with them, and I imagined my parents still together. I imagined finding their faces in the audience, in a crowd, in a church, and I imagined them together.

I imagined the two of them in the front seat of a car and Cody and me in the backseat, playing Botticelli and Ghost and all the other car games our parents loved to play. I saw the four of us, a family, moving into rented beach houses and hotel rooms, traveling through life together. If I closed my eyes and searched my memory hard enough, I could see my parents holding hands, sneaking kisses, sleeping together like spoons. There was no Ava Pomme. No Zoe. It was just the four of us, happy.

But suddenly, kneeling here, I saw my life differently. It would always be fragmented, broken in two. I would find my parents' faces in a crowd, but they would be watching me separately. They would be holding hands with other people. They would be making different lives. And I would always be choosing, taking sides, feeling bad no matter which parent I left behind. My life would be full of train rides that left one of them waving good-bye and one of them waiting for me on the other end.

This wasn't the life I would have chosen for myself. But I saw that my choices lay ahead of me. In this matter, my parents had decided. They had fallen away from each other, and I would forever be somewhere stretched between them.

When my father came and knelt beside me, the church had grown darker still.

"I'm sorry, Madeline," he whispered. "I wish it could have all turned out differently."

That was how I knew I was right. Sometime in my happy past, he had met Ava Pomme and fallen in love, and left Cody and our mother and me. Maybe he had done it because adults believed things only came to you once in a lifetime. Maybe someday he would understand that was not true.

Back in the apartment that night, I climbed into bed with Cody. Asleep, he looked almost like one of the angels in the

Sistine Chapel, and I wanted to wake him up and hug him hard. Instead, I just pressed myself close to him, hating that someday he, too, would figure out what had happened, how our father had betrayed us all. On the walk home, my father didn't say anything, and neither did I. What else was there to say?

In the morning, I woke up to Cody staring right into my face, breathing his morning breath all over me.

"Are you sick or something?" he said. "You smell bad."

I smiled. "I threw up in the restaurant."

"Really?" he said. "Awesome!"

"I want to go home," I said.

"I want Mommy," Cody said.

"Me, too."

Cody studied my face for a minute, then grinned at me. "Was it projectile vomit?" he asked. "Or just regular?"

"Regular," I said. "But gallons." I laughed.

Our father took us alone on the subway to the airport, checked our bags for us, and walked us to the gate where an Alitalia plane would take us home. When I hugged Ava Pomme good-bye at the apartment, I kept my body all stiff, imagining another baby for my father's new family.

On the train, Cody chattered about the pizza he would miss and the spaghetti carbonara, and the pony rides in the little park.

"Next summer we'll do all those things and more," our father said, and his eyes met mine over Cody's head. I wasn't ready yet to forgive him. Maybe in a way I never would. But I knew one thing that adults didn't: Over time things change. Kids don't close the doors the way grown-ups do.

We stopped and bought chocolate in the shape of gladiators for the plane ride. We bought American magazines. Then, finally, we were at the gate.

It was crowded, and I searched for my mother among the people waiting to board the plane. I searched and searched but I could not find her.

Then, I heard her call my name — my mother who knew exactly how to hold me when I cried, how to comfort me when I was sick. "Madeline!" I heard. "Cody!" And I saw our mother running toward us, with her arms already outstretched to take us in.

"Mommy!" Cody shouted, and we both ran into her waiting arms.

I closed my eyes and breathed in the simple smell of my mother.

Without letting go of us, she looked at our father.

"Thank you, Scott," she said, "for getting them back safely."

We kissed our father good-bye. Then, arm in arm with our mother, we walked toward the plane that would take the three of us home. Just once, I glanced back, where my father stood watching. This time, he was the one left behind. But I knew that in my lifetime that role would change from one parent to the other, and that I, Madeline, would always be kissing one of them good-bye, and one of them hello.

This was my life now. It wasn't a life that would get me into sainthood, but I decided that maybe I should concentrate on being a ballerina for now. I would never understand why I got that miracle. Maybe it wasn't for me to understand.

"Hey," my mother said as she settled into the seat between Cody and me, "look what got forwarded to you." She handed me a letter.

While I opened it, she did mother things — tightened Cody's seat belt, made sure my bag was safe under the seat in front of me.

I couldn't believe what I was seeing. The return address on the envelope said *Papa Benedetto XVI, Città del Vaticano, ITALIA.*

"How in the world did you get the Pope to write to you?" my mother asked me.

I opened the letter and laughed. It was written in Italian. I couldn't understand a word.

I looked out the window and watched as the plane lifted into the air. Somewhere below us my father stood, waiting. I lifted my hand and waved good-bye to him as the familiar ache that comes when you leave someone behind settled in. My mother squeezed my hand.

"I missed you," she said. "I missed you like crazy."

"Me, too," I told her. Then I closed my eyes and began to make a list of all the miracles I'd had in my life.

The first one, I thought, was my mother. Of course.